A Primer Of Darksome Intent

Mark Roberts

Order this book online at www.trafford.com
or email orders@trafford.com

Most Trafford titles are also available at major online book retailers.

Printed in Victoria, BC, Canada.

ISBN: 978-1-4269-3162-8 (sc)

ISBN: 978-1-4269-3163-5 (hc)

ISBN: 978-1-4269-3468-1 (e-book)

Library of Congress Control Number: 2010907582

Our mission is to efficiently provide the world's finest, most comprehensive book publishing service, enabling every author to experience success. To find out how to publish your book, your way, and have it available worldwide, visit us online at www.trafford.com

Trafford rev. 7/15/2010

 www.trafford.com

North America & international
toll-free: 1 888 232 4444 (USA & Canada)
phone: 250 383 6864 ♦ fax: 812 355 4082

CONTENTS

AUTHOR'S PREFACE:

So, reader, here we are; greetings and salutations. I've had to spend some time really thinking about the direction I should shoot for in this little introduction. I feel like I should at least offer a mild warning, or tell you to prepare for complete madness. If you get my humor, I might make you laugh. If not, I might offend you. I might lure you in, to some dark secluded place, and scare the crap out of you. I may even paint a wonderful, fantastic dreamscape and then hang you within it. But, and this is important, if I can't stir you to *think*, or at least to acknowledge alternative perspectives you perhaps hadn't fully considered before, then trust me, you've already read way too far; you should probably put this book down and not waste your time. Or, you could consider it a challenge, from me to you, and continue. Take up the gauntlet, so to speak.

That all out of the way, I'll move on. Let's see, I'm forty-seven, I spent the last ten years working for a company that was sold to a larger company who then proceeded to ruin a good business. Naturally, myself, and the fifteen or twenty guys who had been the long-time core of the company and helped build it into what it was, all lost our jobs because the new management wanted to "go another way."

1

So anyone not in alignment with the new way quickly found themselves laid off after years of loyal service and hard work; the new regime out of the closet now, basically a bunch of not so good ol' boys; dollar bill-licking rat-bastards.

So what to do now? I'm banged-up and tired, and I put all my eggs in a basket that was rigged for the bottom to fall out.

Oh, light-bulb turning on; I've spent my entire life writing. Poems, short stories, novel-length efforts; dark fantasy fiction ranging over everything from forgotten, nameless, ancient spirits to alien killing machines and pretty much anything else of a supernatural/horror/ sci-fi/profoundly-twisted genre. I've spent years compiling personal journals of my thoughts, theories, ideas, experiences, expounding on subjects like my Wiccan spirituality, the paranormal, physics and meta-physics; magick, the things beyond what we know, the universe, our very existence.

I've always felt the need to create, to express, experimenting with different forms and means of expression. But up until now it was all just for my own…shall we say 'gratification,' or maybe 'fulfillment?' Or 'peace of mind?'

If I can create a picture, or conjure a mood, or invoke a specific emotion that someone else can see or feel, then that's the true reward, right? Guess again, I need to get paid!

Honestly, the very concept of money, its cancerous, implacable presence in our civilization disgusts me. But being a starving artist is much more difficult when you have a family to think about.

That being said, I guess the point I should be after is this: If you as a reader feel me, that is to say, if you enjoy my style and subject matter, if you can envision the images I'm trying to project for you, then you're in for a helluva ride. And I am obligated to do the Rod Serling bit and act as your guide, to try to give you the basic information you'll need to navigate yourself through my labyrinth.

For, this collection is indeed a 'primer,' the jumping-off point for a voluminous iceberg only buoyed beneath freezing black waves, dead ahead. And this little appetizer, ladies and gentlemen, is just the tip of said iceberg.

The 'darksome intent' would be a hint perhaps at my personal humor. The trick to getting me, to knowing whether to turn left or right in the maze, is to be able to pick out when I'm totally yanking your chain, and when I'm deadly serious. In a glass, combine generous portions of Dennis Leary, Lewis Black, Ron White, Richard Pryor, Hunter S. Thompson, and Cheech and Chong, then hold the glass up to a light and try to peer through that swirling, sarcastic concoction. Reflect, warmly, for a moment, on the things that have influenced your life, either at a personal level or a global one.

Then, bottoms up! If you can get it down before the ice melts, you'll probably do okay. Full steam ahead!

The deeper, truly darker passages are where you'll need to tread cautiously. For, the foundations of these catacombs were excavated by the old masters, the stuff I've always enjoyed reading the most; Lovecraft, Poe, John W. Campbell, Robert Louis Stephenson, Oscar Wilde, Byron, Shelley, T.S. Eliot, Tolkien. I could add easily a dozen more from the 'old school' who had a hand in inspiring and helping flavor my own efforts as a writer.

My personal contemporary favorites are, hands-down, and in this order: Peter Straub, Kim Stanley Robinson, and Dean Koontz.

I could never rave enough about Straub, or the huge influence his books had on my own style and perspective. He really helped instill within me the ability to step back and look at what I write, to circle around it and see it from different angles.

In his book, "In The Night Room," one of Straub's characters, a writer, encounters a supernatural being who tells him that for every book written, there exists, in another realm, one copy that reads the way it was supposed to be written.

That concept struck a very profound chord with me. I found myself going back over decades' worth of my own work, and suddenly I totally got it. I saw the material that I had written the way it should have been written!

Furthermore, Straub's body of work clearly demonstrates to me the truest forms of multi-dimensional story painting. And whether he's describing a sprawling industrial metropolis or a seedy river-town, his vision of the setting and the subsequent characters is always a seamless mold into which he pours the mercurial essence of the precise atmosphere needed to maximize the ambush he's very fluidly setting you up for.

The man's a genius. And it's quite possible that his writing influenced my style and approach more than any of my other favorites.

Kim Stanley Robinson: In my opinion, he most effectively demonstrates what I love and enjoy most about writing, which is mentally painting a physical picture which is related through written or printed language. Language is a writer's canvas, words his paint. A writer's quantum singularity, where his/her energy is transformed completely, is the magickal, infinitesimal point where projected language becomes translated language. Effective technique = the proper understanding of localized gravity.

Robinson masters this technique wonderfully, spellbinding and enveloping a reader with a setting effectively larger at times than the story itself. A landscape becomes a massive, alien character, always brooding in the background. Reading one of his books, a reader very well could be standing on the Antarctic polar ice cap, or surveying a frozen Martian desert. The man didn't win the Hugo and Nebula awards for science fiction for nothin'.

Dean Koontz; the inspirations I get from his books are his consistency and energetic pace. The guy's a never-ending well-spring of flowing ideas. A Koontz story is always original, shifting quickly and smoothly through it's gears and holding the road like a vintage sports car. And, at the end, though you might not be where you thought you'd end up, you always get where you were going. And along the way, he loves to scare the shit out of you.

Anyway, believe me, I'm not so arrogant and full of myself as to think I'm even in the same league as Straub, Koontz, or Kim Stanley Robinson, but if I can have as much fun creating my own vision and developing my technique as I had translating theirs', then that's probably all I ever really wanted to do anyway. And in the off-chance that other people enjoy my work and I can make a living at it, even a humble one, then...very cool!

So, regarding the contents of this primer; the poems I've selected here are some of my favorites, though I've written literally thousands. A lot of the poems included here were either transformed later into actual songs, (I've been a member of several original hard rock bands,) or were songs that I had written and then re-wrote as poems.

Some are just good fun, and others may actually be very dark and personal. Remember, the trick is to get when I'm kidding and when I'm not.

For example; I also included brief excerpts from two full-length novels I plan to publish soon, "Whispering Cove," and "Prophets and Phantoms." One came together really quickly, the other, tediously, over years. Both have upbeat moments of levity, but likewise, both have scenes of utterly dark and fearful confusion and frustration; horror and terror, from the most personal levels to the most general.

Both are fiction, but both have little bits of me scattered through their pages. Things I've experienced or things I've felt passionately about, or things I never understood. Or things I needed to sort out for myself or get off my chest. Both were therapeutic in their own ways, for their own reasons.

Whispering Cove came together very fast. I wanted something quick, simple, and scary as freakin' hell. I got it. It's undergoing a 'final tweaking' at the time of this writing.

Prophets and Phantoms is quite another matter. The setting is the Vietnam War, though it's… not so much a war story. It is a story about scared men, in a scary place; it is about confusion, frustration, misery, and horror; but it's also about the ancient magick and vengeful ghosts of a timeless land. It's about survival, betrayal, and revenge.

Vietnam was the obvious choice for a time and place.. Not only did it offer isolated locale, it was also isolated chronologically. Since it was before my time, I could stay isolated from it. I could hold it in place and form the story around the setting. From the characters' perspective of looking back, I saw all the elements that sealed the choice for me.

It's been finished probably since the late 'nineties, but I've been re-writing and re-tweaking it for the last ten years or more. So I have to stop now. I can't make it any more scary or weird or supernatural or nerve-racking or introspective, any more empathetic for those who actually experienced and endured that particular conflict, my father being one of them. (I have nothing but love, pride, and respect for ya, Dad.) Anyway, maybe I've finally accomplished what I needed to with it, whatever the hell that may have been.

So, reader, all that being said, put on some Led Zeppelin, (or Rachmaninoff,) pour yourself a glass of your favorite beer, wine, or liquor, (I recommend 'Physical Graffiti', a glass of good scotch, and a bong-load of quality herb,) and, I hope, enjoy my work. There's plenty more where this came from.

ANTARES

Burning heart of the celestial scorpion,

Slayer of the Great Hunter;

Ever locked in Death's dance with your quiet companion,

The cool supergiant; stellar lightning to the nebular thunder.

Unforgiving winds draw off your divine beauty,

Beating down your iron soul.

And when, in final exasperation, you loose your ancient fury,

Trembling nights will enshrine your lingering glow.

And having graced the heavens so long,

Which were proud to be so adorned,

The Old Ones will raise your name in song, "Cor Scorpii! Cor Scorpii!"

As all the tribes of the Angels mourn.

A COLD DAY

In my search for some promised peace,

Did I stumble and lose my way?

Holy Land? A sword seeks only

An enemy to fight in these distant wastes.

The path I've walked has been righteous enough,

But it's an *eldritch* voice that screams now my name.

"Do as you will, avenger,

Temper thee now neither your mettle nor your flame..."

Seems so long ago now, I lost my heart in a crumbling tenement,

Then, in the mountains, losing my mind.

Born again, a ghost on a hot, dusky wind;

True-hearted and stalwart, I shall hold this line.

So if I meet my maker too soon,

Brother, wish me well;

The blood spilled on these sands will splash the desert moon,

And it will be a cold day in someone's version of hell…

(Some nether region perhaps to conquer as my own.)

APOLLO'S BANE

There you sit, so fine, beyond a poet's best,

The sun's never shone as sweetly as in your eyes.

The first time I beheld you, I knew that a dream

Was never painted as lovely as your smile.

But the world, it is what it is,

And you and I, we're just here.

And what could be might never be, unless…

I tried to just be your friend, and allow nothing more,

Knowing that would never feel right.

I tried so hard to pretend, but as sure as the stars in the sky

I have surely lost that fight.

But the world, it is what it is,

And you and I, we're just here.

And what could be might never be, unless…

All I know is that

The nights are growing colder.

And every morning

I feel just a little older.

I'm so tired of believing

That anything is real,

And the pain of wounds

That Time will never heal.

But I want you and I need you;

If this is love, it's killing me,

Methodically, slowly,

Deliberately, mercilessly…

All else fades to nothingness.

'CAN'T FIND ME

Gliding oblivious

Through the mists along the lane.

Shrouded moon above,

A luminous membrane.

There is only me now;

The night sky melts away.

Don't think I ever came back

From those astral planes.

All around, the gnarled forest,

Holding fast it's secrets;

Bending, thrashing branches

Hide and protect me where I'm sleeping.

Wearied, resting; was I so unswerving

With the Time I *had* to burn?

You blame me,

I'll blame you.

Wherever could I have gotten to?

You'll never find me here.

CHIEFTAIN

Our banners glorious, the red of blood,
Like the shores of Anglessey.
Quietly, through the centuries, we have endured;
The children of the groves, Blessed are we.

The Lady, her tears never drying, waits patiently
For the wayward to awaken and find their way back home;
Where the Green Man roams free
And the brook whispers to the stone.

Yet, a darkness seeks to consume this world;
The shrieking, snarling beast which Man has spawned.
A juggernaut, spewing lies, greed, corruption, ignorance, war,
Bearing down like an angered cyclone.

And though we are battered by an out-stretched leathery wing,
Our truths will always haunt the irreverent.
And echoing forever over the rubble and devastation,
Our song will drive them to madness.

Mighty old oak, Duir, ancient chieftain,
The only thing left standing true,
Amid man's folly, in the smoke and ruin,
Beneath a sky that can't remember blue.

Our banners glorious, the red of blood,
Like the shores of Anglessey.
Quietly, through the centuries, we have endured;
The children of the groves, Blessed are we.

CROCODILE MILE

All the herd, thunder on the road
To the watering hole.
You'd better check your shit now,
Make sure it's all working straight.
Then you can put the fire to the bone.
(And I've got my seventy-one dollars on...)

All the crocodiles, waiting in the bush,
For the ones who see too late;
Speed on by, man, you're just in time for the big snap,
When they come sliding off the bank.
(And I've got my eighty-five dollars on...)

All down the river, man, I'll tell you these damned leeches
They suck a poor boy's blood.
All down the river, thundering hooves;
The herd is on the run.
(And I've got my 'hundred-and-one dollars on...)

Hey there, you fucking Dudley; bright, shiny teeth,
And that bright, shiny gun.
Get ready now, here comes the big game;
It's five o'clock and the feeding frenzy is on.
(And I've got my 'hundred-and-twenty-four dollars on...)

DIAMOND IN THE SAND

Being alone...means *to be* alone. To be alone by choice indulges the need to brood. To be alone by circumstance substantiates that brooding. Either way, the sudden realization that you've grown used to being alone can be a very scary one.

And Time is then truly that sinister phantom sliding quietly in and out of the wispy dream-mists of a forgotten back-country; the ether fabric of a dark nether region where the sun hasn't shined in eons.

Lovers will come and go, and then they're only faces in a crowd again. And Time all the while stands perfectly, solemnly still, indifferently watching a world fade and die, it's dreams and ideals falling into ruin, consumed by the sands of a lifeless wasteland.

And the Soul, the *core-magick,* freezes to cold, hard stone; a great sarsen, a Watcher, waiting, wondering if anyone will ever come to dig the sand away.

But Time is a bastard. Time feels nothing, it knows no emotion, it offers no sympathy. It just waits for the Watcher to die. There are no miracles here. Just Time, and the Watcher, and the voracious, eager sands.

And so, Time just waits. Merciless desert winds whip the Watcher's stone face with the stinging sand. Great stone eyes squint against the storm, struggling to maintain some vision. But dreams, for so long the only visible landmarks in the distance are gone now, swallowed up. And this unrelenting sirocco is fierce, unbearable. The great stone eyes fall shut.

Is this then, surrender? Are dreams gone forever, utterly, suffocated in the sands? And what for the soul, the great stone Watcher? Eyes shut tight now against the storm, did he come so far, endure so much, questing for something real, something pure and sacred, (the Dream?) only to meet defeat so inconsequentially in these desolated wastes?

His agonized defiance is sealed within a silent scream now, locked within the stone, *within himself.* Too blasted and whipped by the storm to stand fast any longer; stalwartness near ready to bow to subjugation.

Blinded, too weak to open, the great stone eyes can't focus at hopeful distance anymore. And the weight of the sands feels too deep and crushing to ever be dug away. Is this, then, surrender? Unconditional, no terms, no treaties, no fanfare, sand has swallowed everything while Time the bastard just stood by waiting?!!

No. Ironically, (cue quavering laughter,) this can be only a stalemate. The Watcher cannot protect the dreams, but neither can Time strip them away. The dreams persevere, ever abiding the crushing sands. And so the Watcher, sensing lee behind the chance shift of a dune, sleeps.

In Time's camp, a frustrated head of steam begins to build. For, in all it's infinite sovereignty, Time is powerless while the Watcher sleeps. It can do nothing, just hang out, waiting, a fuming vulture in a dead tree. And the Watcher sleeps and sleeps…

…A dark millennium comes and goes…There has been no single ray of sunlight upon this wasteland for a thousand years…But suddenly, the great stone eyes flicker open. Then open wide. Oh yeah, snoozing for a thousand still, quiet years of dreamscapes forgotten? And suddenly snapped wide awake, as if slapped hard by…what? A gasping glimpse of hope? A dim glimmer of something both refreshingly familiar and frightfully distant…a worthy miracle, struggling to draw breath?

"No way, there are no miracles here," says Time, flapping it's vulture's wings now.

Oh yeah, the Watcher is very awake and aware now. Where are my dreams? Those simple dreams of Truth, Beauty, and Peace, that once were the very blood in my veins? Buried beneath the swirled sands, waiting to be wrenched free?

And is that a frail ray of sunlight creeping into the sky? A sky which has been only a dull, bleak grayness for a millennium? And what's that sparkle there, growing brighter, more alive, as a newborn wind gently blows back the sand.

There it is, Time, you bastard, look for yourself. A bright, fragile gemstone, gleaming like the dawn of a new age. There is my dream. Alive. Radiant. Brilliant. After all that; lovers and sandstorms and silent screams locked in stone and waiting vultures and a millennium's sleep, there it is.

My diamond in the sands.

AN ESSAY ON

INTER-PANTHEON RELATIVITY

[Author's note: This 'essay' is actually a preface to a life-long work in progress entitled "Seeking True Magick," *a treatise/manuscript effort aimed at compiling and summarizing my personal journals. I began writing down my thoughts, theories, beliefs, experiences, and ideas probably somewhere around eleven or twelve years old, on the things that seemed most important to me; the Arts, Science, Philosophy, and Religion. The result is demonstrative of how I arrived at these ideas, a sort of how-to manual for helping condition the human mind to be open, aware;* per-*ceptive and* re-*ceptive;* "See through bullshit and get right to the heart of things." *That's one of the most important 'cardinal rules to live by' I've established for myself.*

"Seeking True Magick" also describes what I sometimes jokingly refer to as my personally hot-rodded approach to Magick and trying to understand The Mysteries. I've been shown many wonders.*]*

Baruch de Spinoza, a seventeenth-century Dutch philosopher, (an excommunicated Portugese Jew,) is remembered as one of the great Rationalists. His deistic and pantheistic beliefs became early cornerstones for me, key in formulating my own philosophical views, and meshing perfectly and fundamentally with my preference for ancient Celtic and various other forms of relevant mysticism.

God is Nature, and vice-versa. And everything there is exists only as aspects or parts of the great whole that is Nature, God; our universe.

If one studies the general base concepts of Wicca it is relatively easy to find the underlying root themes that should readily unite all peoples of all religions. Of course, it could never be that simple. (Sigh.)

The mainstream religions, [that is, the ones creating most of the social and geopolitical problems of the world today, you know, the brain-washed, stubborn fanatics and extremists, brandishing obsolete motivations and armed with intolerance and passionate hatred; yeah, those guys,] would rather be separate and exclude themselves on the grounds that their beliefs above all others are correct and true. Their interpretation of "God" is the only interpretation. Well…aren't you special?

Wake up, bone-heads. You're screwing things up for the rest of us. I'm about to show you how to cut to the chase.

All Gods and/or Goddesses are simply aspects, as we humans perceive them, either by cultural tradition or geological ethnic custom, of the One God/Goddess, the 'One' being of both male and female attributes, the physical and the spiritual, the yin, the yang, all combining to make up the Great Whole, all that is: Nature.

And the direct communication line by which we are all connected to each and every thing is the life-energy within us, the human mind. The same electricity which physically fires our neurons lights the massive structure of inner consciousness. Along this current we may also find all our deities and demigods.

Though as individuals our minds, the place where our souls reside, may at times feel like our own tranquil, spartan, little room, (or a lonely chamber of horrors,) the life-energy place also has a door opening inward on the realm of the metaphysical. And the corridor it opens to connects all other doorways, everywhere.

Inward is where we are our true essence. Inward is where we truly see, perceive, visualize, realize, and understand. Inward is where we are one with everything there is; the underlying electrical current; Magick. Nature.

Imagine yourself leaving your personal little chamber, moving down the corridor, (or conduit, if you prefer.) Imagine what's behind all those other doors.

Follow the gradually spiraling, rising, conduit until you find yourself ultimately deposited in the center of a vast open circular arena, looking up at a great united congress of abiding dignitaries; The Old Ones, representative of all human religious and spiritual experience.

Our individual aspects of human spirit are here, the center of the arena; the hub, or center of an individual's life-wheel. And the spokes are connecting corridors, (the magickal conduits,) by which we are connected to "God;" the intelligence and purpose that animates all existence and every thing that exists.

And the outer rim is the High Place, the outer reaches of this next realm; the seating sections of the arena where abide all the pantheons of gods and deities we humans have organized and named historically and geographically through the communion of belief, faith, and worship. We acknowledge the High Place and it's inhabitants, thus completing a circuit; our role in the equation of symbiotic relationships between aspects of the great whole.

We substantiate and sustain our gods, our magickal deities, and vice-versa. The current flows through the conduit in both directions. It gives, it takes, it is perpetual, uninterrupted.

So take a moment, meditate, envision yourself in that colossal arena, gazing up at the Old Ones. Greet them up in the High Place and introduce yourself to them each in turn in their seating sections.

In one realm for example, abide the ancient traditions of various Celtic Gods and Goddesses, inclusive of all the honored heroes and demigods and various other types of entities and beings, which were prevalent in a much broader geographic area and time-frame than most people realize. You could even break these general traditions down to specific regions or tribes, depending on your preference or purpose. You might relate to ancient Gaelic or Welsh beliefs, or maybe the deities of, say, the Norse, or other Scandinavian or Germanic tribes.

In adjacent sectors of the arena's bleachers may be the ancient Greek gods; or the Roman pantheon, or Egyptian, or Hindu, or Native American, or Babylonian, etc. And each also on their thrones, all the figureheads, heroes, saints, and sages, immemorialized by human experience and faith; Buddha, Confucius, Jesus, Muhammad; Jews, Christians, Muslims, Taoists, Wiccans; Allah, Jehovah, Odin, Cernunnos. Everybody's at this party.

And if we trace deeply the roots of all these traditions and examine closely their most basic underlying concepts we quickly find that many of them have a lot of very specific ideas and characteristics in common, demonstrating that ancient pantheons completely separated by locale and time can be very much inter-related by ideology.

Some even share specific symbols and deities.

For example, in many cultures mystical and spiritual importance is often attached to certain numbers, or the idea of simple harmony and balance with Nature. The hierarchy of Catholicism recognizes and lists demons originating from the ancient Babylonian and Assyrian cultures among others. And some Christian Saints originated as Celtic deities, euhemeristically adopted by early Christian missionaries in their efforts to convert the Celtic peoples, much as they established holy days to coincide with pagan festivals, and borrowed the pentagram (five-pointed star) to symbolize the Five Wounds of Christ.

East Asian philosophies often express and demonstrate spiritual and mystical concepts in "triple essences," symbolism expressing, in three distinct aspects, an ideology united or intertwined as a whole. The ancient Tai Chi symbol (Yin-Yang) surrounded by the eight tri-grams (Bagua) symbolize all that is Heaven and Earth and Spirit, each tri-gram, (groups of three stacked horizontal lines, solid or broken,) depicting a spiritual state, a physical attribute, and a correlating element in Nature. The Yin-Yang symbol itself does represent harmonic balance, but balance of the universe as a whole.

All there is, physical and spiritual, positive and negative, masculine and feminine, all energies, all elements, all transitional states, are united and interdependent as the One whole.

We can take this ideology and compare it to ancient Celtic beliefs for example, (and those of many other cultures or religious systems,) and find specific direct correlations and consistencies. The Celts expressed many of their ideas and concepts in tri-grams or triads as well. The "Triple Goddess" for example relates the feminine energy of a Great Goddess as being made up of three aspects, the Maiden, the Mother, and the Crone. And one of the most prevalent underlying concepts of

Celtic belief was harmony and balance with Nature, the Elements, our cosmos.

As a final demonstration of how specific ideas and symbolism are often shared by distinctly different cultures, do a minimal bit of easy research. Compare the ancient Asian symbol of the Samtaeguk, ("Triple Supreme Ultimate,") and the ancient Celtic Triskele. They're virtually identical in form and represent summarily the same relationships between the energies of existence.

The various religious traditions as they are presented today have come down to us molded by history, mutated over time, and as interpreted by cultures who gained prevalence largely by expansion; conquering their neighbors. The actual realization of that fact is the first real step towards true enlightenment.

Why was the gospel of Mary not included in the Bible? It related, after all, what were supposed to be direct intimate teachings of Jesus Christ. Was it because these lessons represented a more gnostic side of Jesus, as he indicated that esoteric knowledge and understanding are the keys to salvation, and that God is the life-energy within us?

Likewise, many texts and gospels that would have seemed very centrally relevant were excluded much for the same reasons. They varied from the prevailing Hebrew or Judaeo-Christian allowances, as established by their interpretation of a "God" figure who, at times, (it seems to me,) is revealed as very jealous, vengeful, and intolerant. Way to set an example, Dude.

Hypocritically sanctimonious pretentiousness only breeds fanaticism, prejudice, hatred, and violence. And once these conditions gain prevalence, initiating pretty much the ultimate corruption of any belief in the Divine, how does a global community rid itself of this cancer, this stain?

The place where a religion fails and begins to break down is the point where it's practitioners and followers misinterpret and corrupt it. And that occurs through the inevitable pretense-fortified human interactions within the physical world.

Undisciplined emotionalism is easily camouflaged within extremism. Hence, irrational fanatics are the product of the corruption they can't or won't see concealed within their ranks and often at the roots of a tradition bent to history's own preferential perspective. In the spiritual, inner world this break-down point is a tradition's structural failing. In the physical, outer world, this anomaly manifests it's negative nature and attributes as Intolerance. And at that point anyone or any people with differing beliefs or perspectives are regarded with animosity and dismissed as holding inferior, or unworthy, unclean stations; we blasphemous heretics, pagans, infidels, and sinners.

To any seeking true enlightenment, or "True Magick," heed these necessities: Open your eyes, open your ears, open your heart, soul, and mind.

If blind faith isn't working for you, or, more directly, if you feel like you've been conditioned to be locked into a belief or faith by tradition, or by the social pressures of your environment or upbringing, throw off that yoke; Conceive, imagine, actualize...see!

"God" is within each of us, and within is where our answers lie. Seek, and, unless you're a brain-washed, fanatical, sociopath, ye shall find. Reach out and "Part the Mists."

FOREVER ENCHANTED

My first glimpse of you
Was in a dream long ago;
But I knew, when I saw you again, beyond any doubt,
That I had loved you before;

Through so many lifetimes, through
Darker times, and times of feasting.
My heart would weep for Eternity
If I ever let you down.

I know that I would happily die a thousand deaths,
If it meant each time I would find you again.
To you, I could never lie, my soul, my world, they are you,
The One who sees within.

I've known great tempests
Born from deep within your passions;
Ages untold I've been under your spell,
The Goddess whispering in your every kiss.

Again and again,
I will lay my sword at your feet;
Do with my heart what you will,
Again and again, each time we meet.

I'm forever enchanted,
By a smile, bewitched;
A longing far surpassing the romantic,
Burning, consuming, timeless.

Forever enchanted,
Lost within the softness of your eyes;
The fire of our magick,
Warming the coldest night.

Forever graced in your presence,
And charmed by the music of your voice;
Like the Sun ever following the Moon,
Knowing that I've never had a choice.

Forever enchanted,
Bound to an inexorable truth;
Every song my heart sings
Is only for you.

THE GLASS STAIRS

Carefully, down fragile stairs, my lightest step,
To that massive door, barred and double-bolted against the demons
there;
Again, in my dreamscape I have come, as I knew I would,
But now that I'm here, do I dare?

Though there is no light beyond, I know what lurks
Down in those dilapidated catacombs, waiting;
My fears, my hells, and the monsters which within them dwell,
And dank, cold, darkness; alert, uncoiling…

Above, a distant world lets me go, and I leap down from it's grasp,
For I will be slave only to my own free-will.
Unbarring the door now to this, my own tomb,
Cleverly, I have ditched my oracle.

How tranquil, this level of abandon, how perfect the blindness,
How sensuous the utter uncertainty.
Complete serenity numbs any misgivings now;
Steeled within resolve, forward to meet the enemy.

Only here can we be square and equal, for above or below
There is only complete madness;
This dark place is our only common ground, and
Behind me, the glass stairs are shattered.

ILL-FATED

For weeks, as we've sailed, in my dreams she comes on the night,
Peering through my portal pane;
Dancing on the moonbeams which paint the rolling sea,
So softly crooning my name.

Siren, I hear you calling me...

On this night, a she-devil, risen again,
Comes to claim my soul;
Wretched sea-witch, calling to me,
And I grow weaker, I know.

Calling down her fury
From the gods of the sea,
And I am helpless, enraptured,
Her ceaseless song entrancing me.

By terror my eyes are stricken now,
As nightmare unfolds.
For she is one I already know,
From misadventure tales ever-told.
She sings to me
And the swells begin to toss.
All about, the tempest rages,
Surely we are lost.

Siren, I am on my knee,
And my ship is yours;
We ill-fated voyagers
Doomed for a watery grave like so many before.

Siren, deceiving seductress,
Let the deep claim us all then;
My brave crew, I am sorry,
We shall not see home again.

The helmsman screams
His surrender to the sea,
For he knows from the Siren's song
There is no release.

My ship now broken in splintered ruin,
Smashed upon the reef;
Now at last, Siren,
Do as you will with me.

INTERLUDE

The world goes crazy,
The same time every day;
Everything turns acrylic,
And the temptress sways.
Seining this sea,
They harvest only madness;
Grating my bubble
Where I am so lawless.

The masses orgy,
It's an ugly chase;
Broken trusts
And indifference to disgrace.
Dodging and evading,
I can keep them at bay,
To resurrect you once more
And make good our escape.

But, soon enough, I know,
Once more we'll set each other free.
And for fleeting moments, all will be
'As above, so below,' if only so briefly.
Again, the streaming sky above
Seduces and intoxicates us;
Still warm, the smooth pavement
Accommodatingly awaits us.

The gauges mirror your sighs, your elegant splendor,
We're revved-up and clean.
Eagerly, you respond to my desire,
My girl, my machine.
Acceleration, not unlike making love;
We're immodest and brazen.
Windows down, not unlike abandon,
Our interlude; we fly for the horizon.

INTO THE DEEP FRIED BLUE

A tip of the hat to all the fascists,
Snuggled in bed with *Big Money* whores;
You've coaxed the sheep into the pen,
Go ahead and slam the door.

But some of us never followed,
We prefer the green of the fields;
And though all around may conspire the wolves,
We will never yield.

Lazy summer days, like a livelihood,
Found and then taken away.
You chumped us into playing your game,
And then we were betrayed.

But I never wanted to play anyway,
And your lies are wasted on me.
I haven't the time to be blind,
I'm busy being *free*.

I'll ride the clouds to 'far away'
It's always 4:20 somewhere, *don't you know?*
So, 'later days,' I'm leaving you behind,
Somewhere far below.

We are a chorus of love and laughter,
We are happy stories told.
But for you the 'war' is over,
Ashes to ashes, we drop you in your hole.

Into the deep fried blue,
We'll fly without you.
And, as your era fades behind us, we'll know,
Your sea of lies has finally drowned you.

KICKIN' IT WITH THE BOOGEYMAN

Dance not with the mamba,
If you don't want to feel the bite;
He's got your name, he's got your number,
Next he'll have your life.

The shadows tremble to the beat of drums,
The boogeyman, he's coming tonight.
The jungle's rockin', and the boys in the band,
They know they better get it right.

Dance not with the mamba,
If you don't want to feel the bite;
He's going to come creepin' in through your window
In the dead of the night.

Me? I'm just kickin' it with the Boogeyman,
Bare feet dancing in the sand;
"Boog-a-loo" said the Boogeyman,
"Spread this voodoo across the land."

LOVE-JACKED

Heavy is my heart
For the poison you must swallow;
But in darkness you'll find my light,
And you know you will follow.

Follow a madman into these badlands
And lay bare your darkest dreams;
Follow a shooting star into the heavens,
But pray for the sound of angels' wings.

Lost now is any horizon,
Forgotten, all our reason;
Tainted are our souls
And cold is death's season.

And if we thought life wasn't long enough,
Did we really think it could end?
So much at our fingertips,
As the journey it only begins.

THE MAGUS

Fixed upon it's chain, prismatic, reflective in the soft light,
From my finger dangles the amulet.
The Mother-stone, one of The Three, the vault which keeps my ideals;
The library of my essence.

Perched here am I, high in this tower, my secret world, my sanctum,
Where ancient runes roll on an incorporeal sea;
Immersed in the science of Nature, whose secret depths I have known
As I swam the eddying mysteries.

Many understandings do I possess: Good, Evil, Darkness, and
Illumination;
A higher universe of new dimensions only we few can know.
Beyond the singularity, where the Old Ones dwell,
The timeless realm where only we few can go.

And if a wary eye spies my quick shadow, high in a slit in the stone,
"Look there, it's that wily old caster of spells!" they'll say;
Tongues that could scarcely articulate neither the cosmic tapestries I
weave,
Nor the plane where my thoughts work and play.

We are the Order of the Magi, invokers of enigma,
Challengers to Time, steadying an unsound matrix;
Of the highest covenant, inhabiting a realm of secrets,
Siblings to the Elementals, conquerors of the paradox.

Misunderstood

I still have the treasured mementos and timeless photographs, symbols of the golden friendships of youth. And I still listen to the magicking, vociferous music that was to be our own unique timbre, the guiding soundtrack on our mission to change the world. Weren't we such inspired, uninhibited bohemians? In our most shining moments, propining, benevolent, humanitarian, visionary, and romanticizing. At our worst, the Lady Caroline might have referred to us as *"mad, bad, and dangerous to know."*

Life had quickly granted us vast troves of treasure: freedoms, pleasures, arts, and the unique, innermost gifts we each possessed. Logic, passion, empathy, imagination; *Enchantment, Clairvoyance, Precognition.*

And maybe we did kick some ass for a while. Maybe we truly stood up, raised our fists, and were counted for what we believed in. And then they herded us into the corral and eased the gate shut behind us, locking us in with the economic sanctions of a fascist elitism and the brutalizing weight of social punishment and persecution. All in the name of their sanctimonious propaganda.

How strongly I believed in friendship, the fervent bondings within our impassioned youth and naivete'. Nothing else in our world mattered as much. We ran wild and lived free and barefoot. We dared to explore, and perhaps we thrived on uncertainty. We fought valiantly for our beliefs, often to the point of self-destruction, but were inevitably overwhelmed and overrun.

For, as quick and generous as Life had been to offer up it's treasures, lulling us with illusion, it turns out it was just as eager to serve us up a wide variety of gripping addictions to choose from, both physiological and psychological. And we, of course, being indestructible, each rushed headlong into the waiting arms of our own demons.

In retrospective reflection, I sometimes wonder at the miracle that I'm still alive; so many of our brothers and sisters are not. Fast cars, impulsive decisions; a veritable smorgasbord of drugs and alcohol, ever at our disposable; greed, lust, jealousy, desperation, ever gnawing at the fringes of our psyches. Our armor began to fail us. What had once been a care-free romp of exploration darkened easily once we began to test the potential range and truest depths of our liberties and freedoms.

Hell, it's a wonder any of us are still alive. And though I had to give up the drugs a long time ago, there must still be some mischievous, giggling part of me that enjoyed every gut-wrenching, teeth-grinding moment of my folly. And an even more certain part of me will argue forever the pro side of a marijuana debate. (Archaic laws, specimen bottles, and the Gestapo of labor, industry, and insurance bureaucrats be damned for their hypocrisy, deceit, and propaganda-campaigns. Fuck you lying, lobbying, manipulating, self-serving, Nazi sons-of-bitches. Don't try to shrug and look all innocent, you know what the fuck I'm talking about.)

Yes, life had once been so sweetly simple. We were thrill-seekers and heretics, one and all. And for a brief, gleaming age, perhaps the truest freedoms were within our reach. But gradually, agonizingly, our most sacred ideals began to blur to tenuousness. The beautiful culture we had forged proved only doomed to suffocation. Our innocence fled.

Our Eden buckled under the weighted shadow of obese, gluttonous sovereignty. (Revolution? Yeah, right; you and me against the Big Guns.) Our desperation sought resolve in futility. The airy chapter of our youth had been allowed us only for the purpose of luring us to the pit, a turgid tome that was Life's own Primer of Darksome Intent. Our Utopia burned before our very eyes.

And then, only after we were securely entrapped, mired in it's tragedy, Life revealed it's tenebrous designs, it's true colors. Suddenly all bets were off. Logic, Intelligence, and Ideals were no longer relevant, an individual's virtues were conveniently forgotten or easily disregarded.

The precognitive dreams and clairvoyant flashes I had once regarded as wondrous gifts became crippling, confusing, no longer to be trusted. What had once been enhanced sight, perception, awareness, became illusory, hallucinatory deception; trickery. And the foot in my mouth ran amock. Had I been forsaken? Or had the perimeter of our sanctity been penetrated?

And even as the echoing crescendo of our brilliant sinfonietta faded in my ears, from the darkness of my angst I realized a truth. There was a putrefying solvent dissolving the past. And even our golden friendships were evaporating. Deny me nothing, and I, the same for you. I guess I misunderstood.

Everything we had forged, all that we treasured and held sacred was slated now for demolition. Forever, it now seemed, was actually only a fleeting, temporary notion, which foundered in the onslaught. All our ideals, all our unshakeable values, all our noble passions and our fearless daring, now only condemned us. Conform, or be damned.

Had it all been just some prank by Life, some bad joke we had been deliberately permitted to play on ourselves, our glorious, defiant insurrection? And I, such a visionary that I had been unable to see the growing cancer poised to consume the future as we perceived it?

The great behemoth awoke. The beast we had heard about, the imminent event we had foolishly thought we understood and were prepared for, reared it's ugly head. The American Dream was at hand!

The whores Government and Capitalism loomed over us now, working in unison to ravish this newest generation of inculpable patrons and infect our collective innocence with the diseases they oozed; greed, corruption, the hunger for power, and the need to legitimize these base agendas. And clutched in their greased vaults, the gleaming, horded treasure; the Golden Apple dangled before us, the ultimate shiny thing: Money.

The worst of those die-hard archaisms conceived in the waybacks of Time's ether which still taints our world today, the one truest bane of our existence, the worst turn our civilization ever made: money. The real golden rule is this: 'The pie is devoured wholly by those possessing the longest arms and deepest gullets.'

Money?!! Really?!! Who even first came up with this concept? History lays the blame on the Lydians or the Phoenicians, or, depending on your definition, even Stone Age Man, innocently enough, it seems, for the sake of convenience. But, naturally, Mankind was able enough to remove innocent practicality from that equation.

One day some fucking genius woke up and asked himself, "Hmm, how can I not only make myself better and more important than everyone else, but also simultaneously create caste-system societies and deny under-privileged people the same levels of education, health care, security, basic comfort, and human rights? What gluttonous conceptual standard can I establish to fuck the world up for thousands of years? Ooh! I've got it!!!"

Son-of-a-bitch. Will our Utopia be forever denied? Will there ever be a world where we can just live, where our truest virtues and individual gifts are our contributions to society? Where the artists can just paint, where the writers can just write, where the violinist can just play, and be as noble and revered, as stable and comfortable, as the aristocrats, industry barons and executives, and royalty and law-givers?

Oh, that's right, I forgot, my vision of what our civilization could be simply by definition negates the conditions that allow for the rise of aristocracies or totalitarian usurpers. But the way we're heading now, not until the freakin' Sun explodes will Power and Privilege be wrenched from the tentacles of the Platinum Octopi.

I mean, really. Even here in our "Great Western Society," the Federal and State governments, so touted as being 'of the people, for the people, and by the people,' have inevitably deteriorated to little more than voracious jack-booted commercial endeavors, omnipotent and out-of-control. More like 'on the people, bending the people over, and sticking it to the people. Oh yeah, did I say 'lying to, and cheating, and robbing the people blind?'

And those long-armed, deep-gulleted, pie devourers have congealed into a great looming, foaming-at-the-maw, bible-waving, sermon-screaming viper, dollar signs in it's lidless eyes, it's puffy jaws swollen with the stinking venom of disguised fascism. And protected in it's massive coils, the Great Lie; the perfect hoax.

'Serve us, feed us, ye mindless minions! Your sole reason for being allowed to exist is to serve the great, lying snake. Play ball with us; compete in our game or be eaten alive!'

The drooling beast, ever-smiling, there beside it's time-clock, the newest whip-cracker, a puppet serving overlords, the Prime Usurpers; the deepest gullets, fussing busily over finance and insurance and pharmaceuticals and oil; the secret rites of the global exploitation of a civilization.

Criminals, liars, and thieves have propped themselves up as the aristocracy, easily granting themselves license and/or immunity, wallowing high above the law, exempt from the cruel and unjust standards they inflict on the drudges below.

All the roses left to wither, all our thorns stripped away.

I think perhaps it was you who misunderstood me. You see, I thought the dream was to be free.

OF HEARTS

Hearts: boiling cauldrons of emotion, passion, and fire;
Old magicians, specialized in confusion and disinformation; the use
of illusion to blind us.
But perhaps, from time to time, in the darkest hours,
They're inclined to shine a light to guide us.

And if the flame proves too weak
'Tis but another wound for a silent veteran;
Alone, brooding at the seaside,
An oblivious tide slowly ebbing.

And if the flame grows warm and bright,
Then once more we are like newborn babes, vulnerable to world and
weather.
But if you understand my heart, and I yours,
In each other may we find shelter.

Every heart, wicked or pure,
Is ultimately it's own heaven or hell.
Every heart is a book filled with both ignorance and wisdom,
Waiting to be read, upon a dusty, cobwebbed shelf.

And every heart is a new frontier, waiting to be explored,
A wonderful treasure hidden deep inside;
It's mysteries revealed when hearts find each other,
Standing together to watch worlds collide.

REVENANT

At the night's heart,
I saw her lonely candle burning;
Wraith-like arms raised to the grove,
Consumed, tempestuous, yearning.

The storm excites her, and she smiles,
Lightning flashes rend the angry sky;
Her scarlet lips murmuring, whispering,
A confused evocation of some forgotten black rite.

The purest extract of evil's sweetest nectar,
The taste of her seduction pulled me in;
But her innocence is a lie easily lent
To a porcelain-white lily in her garden of sin.

Or Deadly Nightshade, dripping, soaked in the pelting rain,
Weeping, her world spinning out of control.
But the cold hands of her familiars come to her, as always,
Yet strangely tangible now,comforting her, caressing her aching soul.

Ghostly specter, above the world she's flying now,
The laughter of madness echoes from everywhere;
'Trick or treat, my pretty,
You're such a lovely scare.'

Giddily, I dance after her, among the gravestones,
Knowingly fueling her wicked delight.
"Come along, then, and play with me," she taunts,
"Come along, to the heart of the night."

RUST

I'm not in the mood for writing pretty verses,
Or to hang twisting in the breeze for too long;
So many truths, *now* coming into focus,
A civilization gone terribly wrong.

And now the weight on *our* shoulders
Is the blood it's going to take to fill *your* shoes;
I thank the Old Ones every day,
That I am not like you.

It's like searching for a vein of silver,
Within a growing darkness;
Seeking beauty in an ugly place,
Or one damned ounce of kindness.

But greed and oppression,
They're needles in a *needle*-stack;
And a mob of smiling liars
Waits to sink the knife into your back.

You can't trust anyone
With the smell of money in the air;
The other end of your bargain,
Do you really think it's going to be there?

And though a super-massive black hole
Steadily swallows up more and more,
Unquenchable burns the fire of our hope
For a peaceful life in a free world.

All of your gold
Can never pay the cost,
For all of the lives wasted,
And the old ways forever lost.

So show me the next dream,
This one's a bust;
And, ol' Iron-fist,
You're starting to rust.

From somewhere without,
A waking whisper stirs a new dawn;
Amid the smoking rubble and ruin,
Could it be, at last, the voice of reason?

SHADOW WALTZ

It's ruinous,
My acute perception of passing time;
Chaos swirls around us,
But still we move in broken rhyme.
Rusting,
My suit of armor, dormant and stained;
As crimson as the drapes and standards adorning the Great Hall,
And the void whispers our names…

It's ethereal,
And we tilt our heads to hear;
Above the storm outside
The banshee's wail is clear.
But, never-ending,
The music plays and on we dance;
Our minds bending,
Pausing just short of every last chance…

It's haunting,
The candlelight that flickers in your eyes;
Gleaming,
The weapons on the wall by which we'd die.
Your body shaking,
Awaiting my release;
In this vacuum chamber,
Forever at peace…

Phantoms at play in an empty dimension
Where Time has never existed at all;
Dancing blindly for annihilation,
Our smiles waver in our shadow waltz.

THE STORY-TELLER

I saw an old man standing on the cobblestones,
His cloak ragged and dusty from the miles of his life;
His body was bent, but his wit was sharp,
And stories of adventure and magick deepened his eyes.

And he spoke with ease and delight of distant, wondrous lands,
Where the sun washed high holy sites.
He spun fantastic tales of honored kings and mighty dragons,
Long-faded glory of days past, and forgotten creatures of night.

Words lighter than the breath of a ghost's whisper,
But with a knowing resonance, louder than his voice;
He spoke of the Light and the Dark like he knew them both well,
Allowing that the path we may walk is each's own choice.

He seemed to have lived for a thousand years,
Relating his life's lessons with fond but wistful remembrance;
"Taught pleasure and *pain without quarter or mercy,"* he said,
"With no source of hope for deliverance."

And as he rambled, his eyes darkening, I could only wonder,
Why impart all this to me?
Until I realized too late his distraction,
And suddenly, I knew his intent clearly.

The lightning of the Ancients burned at the edges of my mind,
The bequest of a legacy I neither understood nor wanted.
And as the old man faded then from *before* my eyes,
I knew at once *too well* where he'd gone…

I'm an old man standing on the cobblestones,
My cloak ragged and dusty from the miles of my life.

SUPERNOVA

A child so blind, misplaced in Time,
Cast coldly upon the Earth.
It's no surprise to analyze what's holy,
All we are *worth*.

Wayward pilgrim, trust your vision,
And the dream you alone may dream;
Elude the Lie, keep hope alive,
Though Truth, you'll find, isn't always what it seems.

'Damned if I know what I'm doing here,
Or how to focus on what's real.
Through this veil of distraction and illusion,
The *Fire* is all I feel.

The *Fire,* can't you see it,
Burning in these eyes?
Calling me home again,
Far beyond these skies;

And when I get there,
Will I remember this place?
I'm flying, hurtling back now,
Am I restored to grace?

...Flying back now, I can hear the Old Ones calling me home...
"Ride the supernova..."

We Blind Pilots (A Short Tangent In Science Fiction:)

Though I can see nothing, I can see everything; the empire I serve, and our supremacy emblazoned in the heavens. Untouchable usurpers, cleansing star-blight. The cables and hoses which lock me into my vision are my life-lines, clutching my gleaming, polished cowling like mother-vines. And, pumped so full of life support, reveling in the bravado and splendor which are my occupational specialty, my every enhanced sense succumbs to the pleasure of our dominion.

My sleek craft hurls me downward and outward, past the Blue Giant, nosing effortlessly into our eighth interior quadrant; my purpose never to veer, the technology at my command never to be denied. The blood that must be spilled to satisfy my payload is but the sustenance of glory.

The twelfth planet flies forward to meet me now. There will I find my prey: Pests, infesting a world no longer theirs; scavengers stealing from the mechanisms we saw fit to erect there; vermin, resisting the inevitability of their extermination, or perhaps simply unable to understand it.

Should I pity them their ignorance? Should I feel emotion, remorse, guilt, for their insignificant life-sparks which I shall soon be extinguishing? Such regret would be blasphemous and weak. Their deaths are mandated by the Empire; that is my mission, my charge.

Breaking through a dense, magnified atmosphere, the great plains rise up, detailed at first only by jutting crags, elevated massifs contoured in subtle shadow. I decelerate, my ship levels off. I can see the long, winding convoy now; a line of activity stretching from our automated installations to the distant pass.

Die now, you vermin who are only damned to do so. I arm my arrays, heating up my emitters. Banking now over the emplacement, I'll begin my assault. Helpless, inferior fools. You've nowhere to run. You're in the open, no cover, no place to hide. You are defenseless weaklings and I am genocide.

I fire, low enough to see them now, scurrying in panic, only now realizing the horror that was always their destiny. Understand now the chaos and uncertainty of death.

My power is inescapable; the wrath of the Empire. A great, flaming tide of charged plasma emission flattens them like a massive, rolling cylinder, smearing them across the abrasive plain. But wait, what's that I spy?

A small group has broken off, fleeing. *Fools!* Grasp now the futility of your efforts. I laugh heartily, feeling like toying with them.

Peeling into a rolling turn, I circle them tightly. We blind pilots have learned to surpass cruelty. Holding my precise orbit, I ring them in cold plasma. Uncharged, it eats away the ground and sucks all the air from within it's range. I can see them now in my ocular sensory implants, writhing, dissolving, suffocating. And my finale? I charge the emitters and fire, igniting the circle. Now they are only smoke and vapor. Back to the main column.

Ah, this is the one soaring joy for which I exist. This is my purpose, my freedom. I am terror, and in my rite I do not allow myself restraint.

Relentlessly, I pound them with fireball fists. None may remain to inhabit these worlds which we claim. There can be only the Empire. Only we are perfection, and none may deny our supremacy. All others are only weak and inferior. They are the star-blight which must be eliminated.

My final pass, emitters on standby. There are no targets left. The terrain below is scorched, crystallized in places. I can feel the residual heat in my life support inputs.

Climb now, my obedient craft. Our mission here is done. Let us return to the Homeworld. Streaking back around the Blue Giant, I deliberately super-charge my engine fields, allowing the giant star's corona to ignite my exhaust signature. It is both a display of vanity, and the indulgence of my ecstasy.

My return trip is pleasant. We blind pilots can fill great voids with self-acknowledgement and soon the interior quadrants of the Empire are sprawled around me. Reaching the Homeworld, I dock my ship and disengage my cowling.

And then I return to my cubicle. All my gear and apparatus are returned to storage, and I prepare to rest until summoned again. I remove my eyes to their container, and resign myself to blackness.

FROM

"WHISPERING COVE,"

THE NOVEL

Karen Chapel sat at her dining room table in her light blue cotton robe, staring out at the bleak morning sky. Grayish white pressed downward, just above the thinning autumn treetops framed in the window over the burgundy metal roof of her Toyota. Her daughter, Gracie, would be getting up soon to get ready for school.

Her husband, Tom, had been called away over an hour ago by Dan Martin, on Sheriff's Department business. Tom had been a deputy for over eight years, but these murders were getting to him, she knew. It was all getting to her, too.

The whole town was on edge, Grand Rivers and Lake City, too. It was all hitting way too close to home. And it all seemed to be centered around Harry Nichols.

She supposed for sentiment's sake she would always have to count Harry as a very dear, old friend. They'd known each other since they were children growing up in Summerland. As teen-agers they had been part of the same close-knit group of friends, partying their youth away on the lakes and down in L.B.L. And for a couple of years, before he'd left for the Army, they had gotten very close. And in the innocence of adolescence, they had drunkenly succumbed to their attraction for one another more than once, and had found deep intimacy in more forms than one.

But even in those happy, youthful times, though he had been idealistic and good-natured, he had been wilder than hell, antsy, unpredictable. And that last summer before he had gone away had darkened and disheartened him in a profound, saddening way.

But life's tragedies and the passage of years had changed them all. And Harry had been away for a long time. Who knew what life might have done to him?

She wondered how well any of them could really know Harry after all these years. He had done a couple of back-to-back stints in the military during the eighties. She had even heard he'd gotten busted for drugs in Europe at some point and had dropped out of sight after that. Then years later he had resurfaced, supposedly living in Denver. After all that, who could really know what he had been doing?

Over the years, she had heard he'd popped in and out for quick visits with his parents from time to time, or when each of his grandparents had died. And there had been a lot of obscure rumors from various sources that may or may not have been true, or may have been over- or under-embellished from one version to the next, who could be sure with hearsay?

And now, after all this time, here he was, with this odd group of strangers, his friends from Colorado. And then there were the murders, although, technically, one had to allow that the first one had been before their arrival. But there was something else about all this mess, something inexplicable that made it so intensely unnerving for Karen. Something just below the surface, laying in wait just for her. And at any moment it was going to burst forth and say 'Boo!'

A loud banging noise behind her gave her such a start she tensed and tweaked her neck in a searing pinch. Gracie's slim, flannel pajama-clad figure shuffled past, headed sleepily for the kitchen cupboard and a bowl of Boo-berry. The loud bang had of course been her bedroom door being flung open and clumsily banged against the wall. Gracie was not a morning person.

"Good morning, hon'," Karen called after her.

Her daughter grumbled something in some untranslatable dialect that only zombies spoke, and her over-sized pink fuzzy slippers continued baby-step cross-country skiing onto the kitchen linoleum. Karen heard a cabinet open, a sliding bowl slipping in sleepy fingers then clattering slightly on the countertop laminate.

A whispered 'shit' as she thought she'd dropped the bowl, and, finally, the cereal box fumbled down from above the refrigerator. The dry morsels poured into the bowl. After a dousing of milk and arming herself with an adequate spoon, Karen heard her skiing back to join her at the dining room table.

Gracie plopped herself down in the wooden chair to Karen's left and sleepily began shoveling cereal, the spoon disappearing with no hurry behind the curly blonde hair that hid most of her face and fell loosely around her slender neck and shoulders. In a subconscious peripheral way, Karen sort of half-noticed the pendant hanging from her neck without focusing on it at first.

"You were out kind of late last night," Karen mentioned calmly.

"I was over at Penny's watching T.V.," Gracie replied between spoons of cereal.

Penny Atherton was Gracie's best friend, but Karen knew this was at best a half-truth. "Or," she added to her daughter's answer, "you were out riding around with Charlie Fulton in that old pick-up truck of his." Her tone didn't change, her voice wasn't raised. She just wanted her daughter to know that she knew.

Gracie drew in a breath that was between a surprised gasp and choking on cereal. "Mom!" Gracie hissed, turning to peer at her now from behind her unkempt blonde locks.

"Oh, *relax,* your dad's not home," Karen shushed her. "Sheriff Martin called him in to work early."

Now Gracie looked her squarely in the eye. "'Someone else dead?" she asked.

"I don't..." A horrified gasp stopped Karen's voice in her throat, all thought processes freezing almost painfully in her brain, as Time blinked for her.

Without remembering standing, she realized her chair was overturned and her coffee was spilled across the table and dribbling onto the hardwood floor. She was covering her mouth with one hand, backing away from Gracie in horror. Her eyes had focused on the amulet around her daughter's neck, and were now locked onto every terrifyingly familiar detail of the small object.

"Mom?" said Gracie, a little frightened now. "What's wrong?"

But Karen was unable to form rational speech, caught in another Time blink. She recognized the pendant, it's oval shape, it's slate-gray color and texture, affixed to the black suede-like tether that Gracie hung different charms and pendants from, depending on her mood.

But this piece was not from her daughter's collection of interesting trinkets. Karen recognized the runic engraving in the center, framed in a Celtic weave-knot border. She understood it's aged, worn condition. She knew full-well it's origin, had seen it too many times in the nightmares her memory had mercifully blocked, but which now came flooding brutally back to her.

Over and over, in her mind's eye, she had seen the object sinking in murky waters. And from the darkest depths, the white hand of Death herself, clawing upward from dark, swaying vegetation to clutch the slowly sinking amulet. And then the nightmare clicked itself into place, back into it's slot in her waking memory. Behind her, a wall halted her horrified retreat from the dining room table.

"Mom? You're scaring me! What's wrong?" Gracie's eyes were open wide now.

Karen stammered, trying to form speech with no voice, so that her response was a raspy whisper. "Where did you get that pendant?".................

"Prophets And Phantoms,"

The Novel

Daybreak; the rain had stopped. Mike Shepherd had been awake for a while, listening to Hahn's shallow breathing in the hole beside him. Could Hahn really be sleeping? The battle of the night before had left Shepherd dead tired, exhausted and burned-out. But residual adrenaline had dissipated very slowly for him. As much as he wanted to turn his thoughts off and try to rest, he couldn't seem to shut his inner circuitry down. He knew somewhere out in the jungle the Phantom was laughing quietly. It had him right where it wanted him. He wondered how Iadonisi was faring.

The re-supply bird came in with ammo and C-rations. No mail. Nor was Isaiah O'Neal onboard. It was just a quick dump-the-shit-and-scram run. They unloaded and lifted off.

And it seemed like the exit of that particular helicopter signaled a change, a metaphysical line-of-departure; one of those defining degrees where another part of each of them died and was born again. Life in the boonies took a nightmarish turn for the really, really bad, as if things could be any worse.

Time was still fractured, askew, and the tempo of all the jerkiness and lurching stepped up to frantic mode. The jungle-rotted depths of their misery and paranoia only intensified the weighty fatigue in their bones. Feet ached like never before. Backs and shoulders were beyond sore and wet clothes chafed against shivering skin. Every man's eyelids were heavy, but the gravity of their collective fear held them captive.

Mid-morning; Lt. Martin and the Recon Platoon had been missing for several hours. From their last known position they could have walked back to the battalion a.o. in less than an hour. And if their radios were all out, they should have been able to signal to any of the choppers that had been searching for them since dawn. Flares, smoke, something. But there was no sign of them.

Alpha Company, being closest to their last known position, was ordered by the Battalion Commander to dispatch patrols to search for them. They found a lot of signs of the enemy's coming and going the evening before, but of Lt. Martin's platoon, nothing.

One patrol even went to the coordinates Martin had called in as the position of their observation post. They found the concealed ravine on the western slope of the ridge and could see the burned hull of the chopper that had gone down in the field below. But still no trace of the Recon element.

At the Battalion Tactical Operations Center, Lt. Col. Butler sipped scalding coffee, but tasted only his tense dismay. Major White was elsewhere, but the Sergeant Major was present and Butler needed his ear to mutter it all out again, if only so he wouldn't be babbling to himself.

"Do you think Martin could have just gotten lost?" Butler asked.

The Battalion Sergeant Major was a big, husky Missourian with earned and won gray hair and a reddish, seasoned face, named Robinson. He had served in Korea and he was on his second tour in Vietnam. He had been to hell and back, and then back to hell again. He felt obligated to state the obvious, which the 'Colonel himself seemed to keep dodging. "What I think, Sir, is that they've been captured." Although the N.V.A. in these highlands weren't usually in the habit of taking prisoners, there was the rumored Viet Cong presence to consider, and they might, if it suited their plans or whims. "Captured or possibly killed," Robinson concluded.

"The whole fucking platoon?" Butler retorted.

By 1300, the battalion, what was left of it, had relocated en masse to the field where the chopper had gone down the evening before. When Charlie Company had lost an entire platoon in battle, that had been a hard enough blow. But they had at least found the bodies, the scene of the fight. Lt. Martin's platoon had simply vanished.

And Lt. Col. Butler was becoming more and more detached and weird as the day dragged along, the mystery going unresolved; a very subtle shift that was perhaps detected by Sergeant Major Robinson, and was perhaps the turning point where things went from bad to worse for him, personally.

He'd seen officers, good men, crack and tilt. Didn't mean they were weak, or flawed. It was just that they'd seen too much, reaching a limit for heedless, unstoppable brutality, the weight of command emotionally blind-siding them.

Butler was quickly becoming consumed, obsessed with finding out what had happened to the missing Recon element. He had determined to stop at nothing, leave no stone unturned. No means to this end would be left unexplored. He ordered his rifle companies to split into platoon-sized patrols and scour the landscape, pushing west in a broad line.

The main trail now faded to an overgrown animal path. As Charlie Company fanned out into the next loch of low-lying jungle before the ridges stepped up again, Third Platoon took the foremost point of the wedge, slogging along the sketchy last traces of the disappearing trail.

At platoon-level, haggard, exhausted grunts knew nothing of the madness that was beginning to take their battalion commander. All Mike Shepherd knew was they were doing a hell of a lot of humping. And the ground under their boots seemed only to be winding higher and higher into hills which were only becoming steeper, suffocated by jungle that grew thicker and thicker. Each step seemed to suck them only farther into more alien, sinister territory, deeper into the death-throes of Time; they could sense the invisible increments of themselves fading, dissolving. The proverbial point-of-no-return had been passed. Nothing that happened after this could be real.

In the distance that grew quickly in jungle this dense, a young private in Alpha Company stepped on something that blew him up. Slightly north, someone on point in Bravo Company snagged a trip-wire. A Bouncing Betty sprang up out of the earth and perforated him with searing death.

But in their green dream-land, Charlie Company pressed on westward, eerily unmolested. To the soldiers of Third Platoon it almost felt like someone, or more like something, was deliberately drawing them deeper into it's lair. They could hear the distant dust-off choppers, first inbound, then out. But, at least thus far, the Phantom had allowed them safe passage.

By now it was around 1430 hours; 'Fuck-You' Bradley walked point. The new lieutenant didn't like him so he'd been fired as R.T.O. and replaced by P.F.C. Benson. Bradley hadn't minded. He certainly didn't like Lt. Turner and he preferred walking point. Though maybe not so much today. For some time now he had felt they were being watched. Were the N.V.A. all around him in the jungle, watching him lead the platoon into an ambush? No, he didn't think so. There was something else.

A couple of times he stopped in the thick bush to peer slowly and deliberately around in all directions. He had to be damned sure he wasn't missing something. Then he would turn to look for Sgt. MacDonald behind him to see if he felt it too. And each time, the look in Mac's eye confirmed his suspicion.

Mac did feel it. Everybody felt it. Nothing was right. Bugs clicked and buzzed, birds called each other, back and forth. And none of it was right. Behind it all there surely must lurk some ominous presence, just out of sight in the jungle's deeper shadows. And after each pause they would exchange a shrug and Mac would motion him on.

Reluctantly, Bradley would wipe his face with the green towel that was always around his neck, then ease cautiously forward. Even though he was extra-watchful now for trip-wires or any other indication of possible booby-traps, the bush had grown so thick that he doubted he could spot much for the wait-a-minute-vines clinging to his damp boots as he inched over the uneven ground. He could barely even make out any semblance of the trail anymore. He could walk straight into the enemy, coming the other way, and not even see them until they were face-to-face.

Behind him, Sgt. MacDonald's senses were wound tight. The underlying tension was surely about to snap. They were in a place where they shouldn't be. The firebase was several kilometers to the southeast. They were beyond even Indian Country now, slipping into an unknown, taboo frontier. These mountain jungles belonged to someone else, beings much older than this conflict of trespassers; the inaudible murmur he sensed haunting this place.

Mac pictured the taut, sour face of Lt. Turner, somewhere behind him in the thick bush. Snidley-fucking-Whiplash. He could almost see him smoothing the points of his villain's moustache. How could the fates have been so cruel as to saddle Third Platoon with this detached, agenda-driven prick?

Lt. Fields had been a good Platoon Leader. Mac had trusted him. These men had trusted him. Fields had been about getting the job done, but the welfare of his men had come first. But, he'd gotten wasted, and his replacement wasn't working out so well.

Mac could still hear their new Platoon Leader bitching them all out earlier. "And another thing, goddamit! If the fucking gooks start yelling shit at you, DO NOT answer them!" He had glared hard at Holliday. "Are you all on dope or do you really have your heads that far up your asses? This isn't a good-will, bull-shitting forum out here! If you hear a gook's voice, KILL HIM! This is a goddamned free-fire zone and he is your ENEMY! Not a buddy to shoot the shit with!"

Hell, at this point Mac didn't even believe the N.V.A. were in the vicinity anymore. He didn't think even they would linger in this spooky, forbidding nowhere-place.

Snidley-fucking-Whiplash. He wondered what this lieutenant's trip was. Turner was no lifer. He may have been once, but not anymore. Something else drove him. Like he had something to prove, or a score to settle.

Mac would keep his eye on him. He would judge and evaluate the lieutenant's every order, his every action, his every move. If he had to assert himself and take command, he would.

Mac hated being in charge, he hated all the coordinating and administrative shit. But at the same time, he couldn't trust anyone else with the fate of these men. 'If you want something done right, do it yourself.' Back on his family's Kansas farm, his Grand-dad had always told him those were words to live by. And here in the Republic of Vietnam, the wisdom in those words had rung true for Mac on numerous occasions.

Towards the rear of Third Platoon's snaking column, Lt. Turner surmised they had crossed a reference point on the map and called in 'Phase Line Sierra.' Captain Andrews acknowledged from the Company Command Post.

Just ahead of Third Platoon the jungle thinned a little, giving way to bamboo and high grass. The high canopy receded, only a hand full of abnormally tall, spindly trees reaching for those heights here, and the steepness of another jungle-choked ridge loomed only a few hundred meters ahead. Bradley turned to look back at Mac again. Another goddamned ridge? Are you seeing this shit?

Mac tightened his jaw. Fuck it. Now that he understood that secretly he had never relinquished command of the platoon to Lt. Turner, he could get on with the business at hand. He signaled wearily to Bradley to make for the base of the ridge.

Bradley turned to look it over again. He wasn't even sure if they were still on the same trail. And the base of the ridge over there was obscured by lonely stands of bamboo and strewn boulders. He straightened his helmet and moved out, low-profiling.

Third Platoon were the ghosts now. They were adapting quickly, matching the spooky isolation of this haunted highland meadow with jungle-Zen. Bradley glided silently through the grass, hugging in close to each new stand of trees or tall, elegant bamboo, as if nestling in soft green curtains which seemed alive and wistful, trembling in the afternoon breeze that eagerly filled the void left by the ceased rain. And the Platoon followed, careful to mimic every stealthy step, zig-zagging across the expanse as if dancing with unseen partners.

Mike Shepherd, low-profiling, gliding jungle-Zen with the best of them; on cue, Isaiah O'Neal's cryptic caution repeated itself in his thoughts. 'This land is full of ghosts.'

'Ghosts and chameleons,' Shepherd quietly allowed to himself, recalling that bizarre dream. He moved quietly toward the next tumble of rocks and bamboo. Look at us now. Chameleons, shape-shifters; we're so far gone how will we ever find our way back?

He crossed the dim path again, and found himself suddenly at the base of the ridge, passing between bluish lichen-covered boulders only to discover the bamboo clambering steeply upward now. We chameleons learn by imitating those around us, those same shape-shifters around him now, moving with an alert preciseness and finely-tuned paranoia; the skills necessary to persevere through exhaustion and numbing misery in this haunted, alien place. And jungle-Zen made them all deadly, the Americans, the N.V.A., hunting each other in a bizarre dance with the land, the vegetation, the ancient spirits of these soaring heights. Prophets and phantoms...

Y BONT (THE BRIDGE)

So long I've wandered this land, ever awash in Nature's cycle.
How well I know her, lain before me, a chart for navigating;
From the snow-pure chill of each passing winter to new vitality and
origin; the rebirth of the forest with each new springtime;
Then the celebration, the festivals, the joy of a cycle in it's sun-lit
prime each passing summer;
Through the inevitable ageing of a Goddess, adored, comforted by a
patron world, her beauty immortalized by autumn's brush-strokes;
But always returning ultimately to the restful hibernation of each
new winter; the sterile white void from whence will spring anew her
perpetual regeneration.

I, the seeker, indulgent of both this Goddess and the fruits I might
chance upon, a mere reflection of her; a mirror of Nature, accepting
the inevitability of my own eternal cycle:
Ever reborn from the snow-pure chill of winter,
Warming, growing with the new vitality of spring,
Feasting, celebrating the festive summer,
Fading inevitably with autumn,
Then on to the restful hibernation of the white void of winter again.

Yet in each rebirth, a seeker navigates a new route over a new land,
chancing upon new fruits. And as I stand at the bridge, the causeway
spanning my subconscious, only uncharted regions lie beyond. I have
but to set my foot forward, and I have taken the first step toward that
new, distant horizon.
But to cross the bridge, and the new journey is begun...

ON A SHORE

On a shore, green plushness softening stone,
We gazed across wide Puget Sound;
Together, yet, in peaceful moments of contemplation, alone.
Then, again she touched me, detached, profound;

Remarking how no two sunsets are ever the same,
Her expression softened in wonder.
An otter played at it's otter game,
And I, like the Sun, struggle hopelessly against going under.

On a shore, a caressing sea comforts stone
Then fractures, shatters, and falls away.
Curious, a tiny bird spies on us from a bush, alone;
And, kissed softly, tiny purple wildflowers float and sway.

Nearby, young rabbits, unafraid of us, bounce in spring grass
And my heart leaps as she returns to me;
Her eyes again dance with her smile, her voice singing as it laughs,
My soul sighs, happy, feeling her beside me.

And I know the otter, and rabbits, and wildflowers
Are there just for us, intoxicated, drunk on Spring.
At ease for a brief moment, relaxed by wine, beers,
We won't let the world mean a thing.

And in our moment things feel clear and right;
Satisfied, the tiny bird takes it's leave.
From the burning horizon, the evening is set alight,
Just for us, on a shore, silhouetted against a shimmering sea.

COLLOQUY

It's a quiet morning, the light from outside is dull and gray, filtering through the plastic I'd covered all the old single-pane windows with back in December. It's May now and the temperature outside has been warm enough I could probably remove the plastic but, like this morning, Washington could yet get a little chilly at times, courtesy of a constant drizzle and overcast sky.

The three big cedar trees clustered in the front yard and their adoring court of rhododendrons are still. The sneaky southwest wind that often sets in overnight this time of year is taking the day off, allowing the rain to be lulling in the sleepy stillness.

Sadie, our giant but sweet-natured Golden Retriever-Irish Setter-Yellow Lab-Husky-mix water buffalo is plopped on the floor looking bummed. She probably won't get to go to the *r-i-v-e-r* today. I tell her she's lucky she's not out plowing a rice paddy like the other buffaloes.

I'm sipping hot green tea, piled into a corner of a living room couch trying to focus on the television, wondering where the hell my glasses are. Across the big, open room, by the stairs up to the second floor, my beloved muse, Kim, is playing a game on the computer, sipping her coffee.

Occupying the corner opposite the stairs are stacks of amplifiers, a drum set, some microphone stands. I think to myself I could have compacted everything better after my band's rehearsal last Saturday. The Judas Priest cover song we're working up pops into my head; "Heading out to the Highway."

I stretch against the back of the couch and turn back to the television. (For a moment the oft-recurring thought returns that I pay way too much for cable.) The program is about sightings of Bigfoot and similar creatures, and the narrator asks something silly, like, "Could these creatures really exist?"

I of course try to engage him. "Do ya think? There's only been thousands of sightings, in 49 of the 50 states."

The narrator ignores me but Kim is ready to take up the issue. "Scientists want to see solid proof, evidence, a body."

Okay, *touche'*. This of course would be the opening point in a debate of this nature. I know she's only drawing me out, her beliefs on the subject being much like mine.

"I remember when I was a kid," I say, recalling some odd incidents from my youth in rural Kentucky. "Something scared my uncle out of the woods. He stopped by our house one morning, after he'd been turkey hunting in 'Land Between the Lakes.'

"He was visibly shaken, and he claimed that there had been something in the woods with him, making sounds like he'd never heard before, grunting and growling and snapping off tree branches. This was a guy who loved hunting and being in the woods and knew every animal in those woods, and he had not wanted to stick around to see what it was. It always made me wonder.

"And," I continue, recalling another odd incident, "I remember one night me and some buddies were out partying, we were out past Iuka at the old Woodsmen's Hall.

"We had parked and got out of the truck, stretching our legs and downing some beers in the gravel lot out front. All of a sudden, from the edge of the dark woods behind the old hall, something ripped off what sounded like a very large tree branch and began making a loud thrashing commotion with it. And then we heard a low, steady, guttural growl. We hastily got in the truck and got the hell out of there."

Next, I begin to relate my only other such personal experience. "And when I lived in the old farmhouse that a buddy of mine had inherited, one night a bunch of us were sitting out on the front porch, six or seven of us, drinking beers. We'd been hanging out for awhile, sitting in the old chairs and the big porch swing, with the porch light on.

"Just at the edge of the area that was illuminated by the light, we could see the front of the old garage about thirty feet away. Suddenly, from a tree in the dark alongside the garage, a limb breaks and we distinctly heard something big coming down out of the tree and then hitting the ground. Then we heard it running off into the dark, a heavy two-footed stride. Something had been sitting up in that tree just watching us.

"Whatever it was," I continue, "had to easily go over a closed gate in a fence, which we heard creaking, before it loped away across a field to evade us.

"Not that we were going to chase after it. But we did load every gun on the premises and stayed up the rest of the night, armed."

"Wow," Kim remarks. My accounts had impressed her. "But, why has no one ever found a body?" she asks again. It is after all a strongly valid point, warranting consideration.

I begin to formulate possible explanations, offering some variants. "Maybe they bury their dead," I say, "or eat them."

Kim grimaces, not appreciating the latter alternative. "Or," I press on, "maybe these Sasquatch creatures are just very ancient spirit-beings who've transcended Time and Space. Maybe they have the ability to shift from one dimension to another, or from one Time continuum to another, and ours is but one of many they inhabit."

She nods, granting me the possibility. "Honey, your theories are endless. Scientists would love to get their hands on you."

I take that ball and run with it. "No, really. I mean, for example, if you examine U.F.O. lore closely, it's obvious that aliens understand and utilize laws of Physics that are way beyond our understanding." (I regard aliens much the same as Bigfoot: There's way too much evidence that suggests there's something going on we have yet to nail down.)

"To cross the vast distances of Inter-stellar Space, *and* given the reported behavior of U.F.O.'s in a lot of sightings, like when they just wink out or disappear, inter-dimensional travel would have to be a reality."

Kim allows my course correction. "Well" she says, "I've never had any kind of 'Bigfoot' experience, but I think me and my cousin saw a U.F.O. once."

I listen with interest as she recounts the experience. "We were driving back over to Spokane one night, on Hwy. 90, and we were just past the Gorge, really in the middle of nowhere.

"We noticed a bright light in the sky and were like, 'what is that?' At first we thought it was a falling star, a meteor or something, but it looked like it was getting brighter or bigger, and coming straight at my car. We were going 'oh my god, is it going to hit my car?'

"Then it came down and went right across the road, right in front of us, a little glowing ball of light." She holds her hands up an estimated distance apart to illustrate the size of the thing, somewhere between a basketball and a bowling ball. "And we tried to see where it went but it was just gone."

"Well," I respond, "it was obviously no meteor. Even a small one, that close, if it hit the earth you would have seen a flash or heard an explosion or something. And meteors don't usually level off to do a fly-by in front of passing motorists. So if it just vanished, that would seem to support my point. Actual physical Inter-dimensional shift or travel has to be possible.

"My guess for an explanation," I postulate, "is it was an alien probe, either from a mother-ship orbiting our planet, or from a different dimension, where it went back to when it vanished."

She laughs, but at the same time she knows I'm perfectly serious. I continue. "It was curious. Two hotties (I've met her cousin,) driving across the eastern Washington plains in the middle of the night? They sent a probe to collect some data and then recalled it."

"Either back to the mother-ship or another dimension," Kim concludes for me, beaming at me with that warm smile.

"Either that or there's a race of really tiny drunken aliens joy-riding around the galaxy trying to pick up chicks," I offer. I'm ready to gather some steam now. The caffeine from my morning tea is kicking in, and Kim's smile is my inspiration. Soapbox here I come.

One of my life's most intriguing anomalies flashes in vivid detail onto my thought-screen. The very clear memory of waking in the middle of the night as a child, to an eerie blue light, almost phosphorous, or having texture, squeezing itself in through my open bedroom window, an angry breeze inflating the curtains to either side.

"I sometimes wonder if I was abducted by aliens when I was a kid."

"I know," Kim says. "You told me about that."

I remember then that I probably had, since we will have been together eight years this summer.

I must have been about ten or eleven at the time because we lived in Sharpe, Kentucky, in Marshall County. The little farm we lived on was just down the road from the Elementary School.

We had a couple of Charolais cows, a bunch of chickens, a 'fainting' goat, (man, did we kids have fun with him,) a very contrary pig, and all the obligatory dogs and cats that kids will require living on a small farm. It was beautiful country and we had a basketball goal and we played in the creek and life was good. But a memory I'll have until I die is of a night when rural tranquility was rent asunder, like soil under the plow of a borrowed tractor.

Could it have been a dream? My dreams are usually at familiar levels of intensity and detail. Even the occasional nightmare is still registered as a dream, the details often fading quickly in the realization. It is because of this one incident, and the fact that I later began to have dreams that were undeniably precognitive or clairvoyant in nature, that I became very alert and aware regarding my dreams, and I learned eventually how to file them. I can tell you, if this was a dream, it was the most inexplicable and realistic dream I've ever had, possessing substance and qualities that dreams should not.

And, if it was a dream, *I dreamt I woke up,* something I've never done since in a dream. I woke up, in the middle of this blue haze, unlike anything I had ever previously imagined or experienced before. And I had never even heard of the possibility of U.F.O. abductions at that age. Not even Hollywood sci-fi efforts of that time could have recreated it. And, there was the violent wind with a life all it's own, on a summer night that had seen no storm.

I snap the screen off, knowing I'll have to summarize to move on. "I still wonder sometimes. If it was only a weird dream, it was the most vivid dream I've ever had. Outside my window there was no road, no source that a light of any kind could be coming from. Just a big open pasture and our neighbor's cows. I guess the cows could have been playing a joke on me, I don't know."

Kim laughs again, that musical laughter that I love.

"What if," I throw out there, "we woke up and found ourselves aboard an alien ship, surrounded by aliens? Would we freak out and try to fight them? Or would we be able to keep our wits about us enough to just try and take in every detail of our surroundings, of how the aliens looked and acted?"

"Well," Kim says, "I think *you* would try to take in every detail. That's just how you are."

"Maybe," I reply. "Until they broke out the probes and surgical instruments. Then, I'm afraid, my disposition would take a turn for the worst."

I'm on my feet then, striding across the room to come closer so I can use body language and facial expressions to enhance my presumed conversation with the aliens. "Keep the fuck back with that shit, I will cave in your big-ass skull, you're telepathic, you know what I'm saying to you."

Amid Kim's laughter, a calico-colored fluff-ball tip-toes into the room from the kitchen archway and sits at my feet, glancing back and forth between us, ready to enter into our discussion at the first opening.

"Nimmers," I greet her in my high-pitched cat-greeting voice. ('Nimmers' is short for Nimue.)

I continue, for my growing audience. "And you know, if this interdimensional means of travel is accessible through mere technology, then how many different life-forms must there be out there advanced enough to have mastered this technology?

"And what types of environments might they have evolved in? Alien life-forms don't necessarily have to be little humanoid shaped beings with big heads. They don't have to be 'little green men' or even 'little gray men.' We've proven here on Earth that Life will form, evolve, and adapt to it's environment even in the most extreme conditions, from frozen tundra to volcanic vents on the ocean floor.

"Even if a planet or moon has a methane-ammonia atmosphere and a quartz crystalline soil, or whatever, if it's located in the right 'sweet spot', orbiting the right type of star, and especially with the right chemical catalyst or the introduction of the right energy process and effect, who's to say what types of life-forms may have been spawned out there in the cosmos, or how different from us they might be? They wouldn't necessarily even have to be carbon-based, or flesh and bone and blood, or even remotely humanoid.

"Aliens might not even have the physiological or chemical ability to understand how human thought and emotional processes work. Their anatomical systems may function in ways our science has yet to understand and acknowledge. And are they then *'in God's image?'*"

"I love you, honey," Kim says, smiling. "You have so many theories about the Universe. If Science could get it's hands on you it could change the way people think."

"That's an underlying principle of how I see our world," I reply. "I wish more than anything we as a people could shed the thousands of years of misinterpreted religious history that has channeled mainstream thought into distorted, out-of –context parameters of perception. The Universe holds endless undreamt-of possibilities for we humans."

Kim readily agrees, (though Nimue is reserving her judgment until she's heard more.) "It *is* too bad so many people are so close-minded," Kim says. "They can only believe what's been passed down to them. They don't understand *how* to be open to other possibilities."

We opt to cross a bridge at this point, from science to religion. "It's just sad that in the 21st century people can still be so unswerving from out-dated modes of thought and perception," I say, stepping across the midpoint of *mainstream*. "And it's not that *what* they believe is wrong, it's just that our civilization's perspective has been hobbled."

Kim stands and moves through the archway into the kitchen to refill her coffee cup. I follow, thinking of going through the kitchen and out to the garage/basement for a cigarette, knowing the timing is about right and she'll follow me out so we can continue the discussion.

We pass through the back door from the kitchen and down the wooden steps. The massive room has a high ceiling and numerous shelves, but it's really neither a garage or a basement. There's no garage-size door nor is it below ground. But the rest of the house is on a raised foundation, giving this lower area in the back an unnamable dimension; 'the big room for laundry, arts and crafts, storage, the furnace, the water heater, the lawn mower, a practice amp and a guitar, some tools and fishing poles, and yet *another* stereo. In crappy weather it's our smoking area away from the kids.

I hop down the steps, past the furnace to the left, then the workbench, littered with paints and brushes, and a propped up painting, a sparse dream-catcher hanging above it, both waiting for me to find the time or serenity to finish them.

We are greeted by 'Tally', (short for Taliesyn,) who has just come in through the secret cat entrance from under the house. Tally is our 'six-toed freak', a desert-sand-tan-colored cat, the oldest of our animals. He slinks twitching across my path.

In his cat's mind he is an ancient puma-god, and we mere mortals are his servants, to command and utilize as he sees fit. And of course we are expected to be ever-vigilant to stand ready to let him in or out either door every five minutes so he can make sure there's food in his bowl.

How far he's come since that day we liberated him from the animal shelter, a tiny, fragile kitten, trembling and freaked out, sitting in the palm of Kim's hand, looking up at me. His fur was all sticking out and fucked-up, I had to laugh out loud. He reminded me of 'Tweak' on "South Park." He looked so pathetic I knew Kim was bringing him home.

I walk past Mr. Puma-god and the washing machine to retrieve my smokes and see what CD I left in the stereo. 'Motorhead,' "Another Perfect Day." I hit 'play' and Lemmy informs someone that whatever they're about to launch into is 'top notch,' then begins pounding out the bass intro to "Back at the Funny Farm."

I had managed to quit smoking for several months awhile back when I got back into Martial Arts, but the stress of tough economical times had lured me back to tobacco a few weeks ago. As I light up, I flash for a moment on a recent e-mail I had received relating that the general consensus is to blame President Obama for the current economy. I sigh. Another case of 'not seeing the Big Picture.' How convenient for everyone that the new guy gets left holding someone else's bag.

Kim descends the steps and takes a seat on the barstool in front of the workbench, producing and lighting her own smoke. Our exodus to the smoking lounge has easily lent enough of a breather in our conversation to allow for another heading change.

She chooses the topic. "Where do you think our spirits go when we die?"

She knows this will present me with no end of possible notions. After pondering for a moment how to articulate my theory, I respond. "I think that, through what is a natural transformation of energy, our spiritual energy goes to the nearest star, our sun. There's been a lot of evidence to suggest that spirits, or ghosts, can either interact with electro-magnetic fields or are themselves some detectable form of electro-magnetic energy.

"It seems logical to me," I continue, "that in that state, spiritual energy would gravitate toward the biggest source of electro-magnetic energy. Or perhaps a spirit is of a photonic energy undetectable in our spectrum of vision, phased to it's own dimensional place.

"Either way, it seems like they would be drawn towards the nearest, most powerful source or manifestation of that energy, and I'd think the Sun would be the strongest source in the neighborhood."

With perfect calculation, Kim inserts the perfect conclusion. "'Come to the light,' right?"

"Oh, yeah," I concede. Good point. "I guess that does make sense," I say.

"But if spirits are supposed to go to the Sun," she says, "why do some stay behind? Are they stuck here?"

I think it over a moment before answering. "Human emotion must be a strong form of energy in it's own right. After all, *we* use that energy in Magick."

I hold my hands out, one palm up, to represent a floor or base, the other as if molding a square shape onto the base. "If where we are now is a box, it's own dimension say, then, once our spiritual energy is freed from our bodies and we are free to move outside this box, it's likely that powerful emotional energy can keep us tethered or tied to this dimension. And a confused or emotionally anguished spirit can't or won't *move on* until it is ready or understands how. And even then, the emotional energy itself can remain behind as a manifestation in the form of residual paranormal activity, like an imprint, stuck in a perpetual loop."

"And how would you define Angels?" Kim asked, expanding on our current topic. "People who've reported near-death experiences often say that Angels or loved ones often appear to try and help them 'toward the light.'"

"I totally believe in Angels," I reply. In the years we've been together, though we've exchanged generalities about beliefs that we shared, we've rarely gotten down to the specifics like this morning. I'm enjoying it, and Angels hold a special place in my beliefs. "I just don't see them in an even remotely traditional Biblical sense."

"Right," she agrees, "it's not like they're the servants of a Biblical God, the old bearded guy on his throne in a 'Heaven.'"

"No," I chuckle. "They're entities whose spiritual energy is in a higher place, a race of beings in a higher existence, like Tolkien's Elves. They are servants of God, but in the sense that God is the Universe. Angels understand their place in existence. We don't."

"I believe everyone has a guardian angel looking out for them," she says.

"Oh, believe me, so do I," I respond. That's why Angels hold such a special place in my beliefs. I reflect for a moment about specific instances throughout my life when, I knew, only a split-second twist of fate, or the divine intervention of a higher guardian had saved my life. And because of those moments that could or should have gone the other way, I often felt like I had some special purpose or mission I was supposed to fulfill or accomplish. "I think Angels, these higher beings, are compelled to try and help us ignorant humans reach a true enlightenment, and are able to take any form they choose, being mindful of human traditions in their interactions with us. Maybe Angels are beings of spiritual energy who, after many incarnations here on Earth, have reached that level of enlightenment. Maybe in every solar system where life has arisen, we'd find the same cycle and evolution of spiritual energy."

"I wonder," she says then, "if your memories and knowledge and feelings stay with your spirit after you die."

"I think so," I offer. "Even though you're only a part or a particle of God, the Great Whole, the Oneness of the Universe, you're still an *individual* particle. And that's the yin and yang of it, a balance that at the same time is the root of all paradox."

She moves closer to me for a warm embrace. "Obviously," she says, "some souls have met before and are destined to meet again," she plants a gentle kiss on my lips, "like us."

"Obviously," I agree with a smile. The first time we met we had each known that it wasn't really the first time. And I had dreamt of her before ever laying eyes on her in this lifetime. I had immediately recalled the specific dream of a couple years before because it was one of those dreams that possessed that special quality and intensity, the kind I had trained myself to pay special attention to and file in a special place in my memories.

She hugged me close again, before stepping over to extinguish the cigarette she had sat in the ashtray. "I'm so glad I have you," she says. "It's like I can talk to you about anything, things I've never been able to talk to anyone about before. That's why we're soul-mates. The way you think is so deep, it's like you not only understand this world, but the 'other' worlds, too."

I laugh. I'm so flattered I'm almost blushing, and doubt that I'm as deep as she gives me credit for. The 'way I think' seems to me to be absurdly simple if anything. "Sometimes, just *because* of how I see things, I feel a little disconnected from this world."

Our smokes finished, Kim decides to take the dog and go over to our friend Margie's house so Sadie can play with her dog, Juneau, and Kim and Margie can hang out for a bit. (Margie is the much-more-agreeable and far-less-facetious 'better half' to Steve, the bass player in our current incarnation of the band.)

I switch off Lemmy and the boys and follow her back up the steps into the main house. When she grabs her car keys, the jingle alerts Sadie.

Her head comes off the floor and her tongue lolls out. Could this crappy day be salvaged after all? Her bushy tail comes to life, sweeping the low nap carpet.

"'Want to go see Margie and Juneau?" Kim teases her.

The beast springs to her gigantic feet, excited and ready to roll. Anything involving a car ride is just good stuff, man. As she bounces and wags, jarring the floor and windows, I realize *she* could be the one leaving all the Bigfoot tracks.

Kim heads out the front door and down the steps to start her car and let it warm up, Sadie bounding out after her. I walk out onto the front porch as Kim is coming back in to grab her purse and a sweatshirt.

Rounding the high cedar fence along our driveway, our neighbor's dog from across the way, Quartz, enters the yard for one of his periodic visits. Sadie of course is barely able to contain herself. She's known Quartz since she was a puppy. For her this day was getting better and better, in spite of the gloomy weather.

Quartz is pure white, part Husky, part Lab, and part wolf, but he looks all wolf. His shoulder sets a little higher than the rest of his back and his fur is coarse and bristly, like a wolf's. At fifteen, he's still a healthy, beautiful animal, though the neighbor says he's deaf. He often escapes and makes a circuit of the neighborhood, surveying his domain and pissing on things. I can sense that he's a wise old soul.

Sadie circles him, nipping and playing as he makes his way straight up to me, like always, for the obligatory pat on the head. I wonder if it's the wolf in him performing some instinctive ritual, regarding me as the alpha male of this yard and asking if it was okay if he urinated on a few things.

"Hiya, Quartz, how are you, buddy? 'Get loose again?" I ask, as if he can hear me. He turns his head a little, so I can scratch behind his ear.

Satisfied that he has my blessing, he turns to go, pisses on a low bush and ambles away in his wolfish gait. Sadie breaks off her efforts at the end of the driveway and Quartz again rounds the end of the cedar fence and is out of our view.

Kim comes back out now with her stuff, giving me another soft kiss. "I love you, 'see you in a little bit."

"I love you, too," I say.

She loads the water buffalo into the back of her car and drives out. I walk over to the lowest hanging branches of the nearest of the big cedars and place my upturned palms against the tips of the flat, scaly fronds and close my eyes for a moment's grounding.

I understand how Sadie had felt a few moments earlier. Despite this gloomy weather and rain this day *is* salvaging itself.

The next day we learn from the neighbor that Quartz has died.

In his honor, we make our way over to the local pub and proceed to get quite sloshed. Goodbye, Quartz, wise old soul. You'll be missed.

WIDOWMAKER

Trusty Colt revolver,
'Peacemaker,' they claim;
But some, I suppose, who've met her
Know her by another name.

We've left a trail of dead men,
In line for the undertaker,
But that's just the way of life,
For me and the Widowmaker.

The hangman is waiting for me,
They're gonna hang me high…

I walk into the saloon,
The Widowmaker, she's by my side;
'Give me bottle of whiskey,'
It's been a long, hot ride.

But my reputation precedes me,
And the price on my head is high;
The sawdust on the floor drinks deep,
As another man dies.

I toss two bits on the bar,
And ride away…

Gunpowder and lead
Are my given right,
And when the Widowmaker speaks,
Someone always dies.

And for the Widowmaker,
There's no remorse for the men she's killed;
And I know that, one day, I'll be there, too,
Lying dead up on Boot Hill.

And the Widowmaker, she won't feel a thing,
As she takes another life.

IF I DON"T SEE YOU AGAIN

I know it's crazy,
Living in the past,
Even though I knew
That we'd never last.

But sometimes I hate you,
Though it really was a blast;
A summertime love
That found wintertime too fast.

So, my, my, here you are
In my face again;
My darkest nightmare,
Risen from the dead.

Crawl, crawl, little viper,
Back into my bed;
I've grown immune to your venom,
That stone has been bled.

The way you put the bite on me,
Left me hurt and sore;
But, believe me, I got mine,
And I'll get some more.

And I'm glad you found it so easy,
Bringing my world to it's knees;
Feel free to make it the last time
The next time that you leave.

So thanks for nothing, baby,
And you've heard this before:
Don't get busted
On the ass by the door.

And, If I don't see you again,
 Fuck ya, baby;
And if do, until then,
I'll always have your knife in my back…to remember 'love.'

THE HEART OF ALL THINGS

[Author's note: The ancient "Irish Triads" have been passed down for centuries, and were eventually included in several old manuscripts, which date as far back as the fourteenth century. Historians speculate that many of these traditions may have even been handed down from as far back as the ancient Celts. Translated, my favorite, which I've found referenced in many sources, is this one: "Three candles that illumine every darkness: Knowledge, Nature, and Truth." I reference it in the following poem, which I've restructured from a song I wrote:]

Don't you linger too long,
Down by the crossroads,
'Cause you just might get what you wish for.

Don't walk in shadow,
If it's light that you're seeking;
You'll only find what you're after
At the heart of all things...

There are just three things,
That light every darkness,
And if you think real hard, you know what they are.

'Knowledge' of yourself
Is to know more than you may think;
That's the 'Nature' of the 'Truth' you will find,
At the heart of all things...

So you see now, your heart
Links you to all things,
And what you give you will receive.

Both wise men and fools understand,
Your eyes must be open to truly see;
Then, you may find your own heart,
At the heart of all things...

Though it might lead you down a lonely road,
wondering where your vision's gone;
Or the life that used to be your own,
Laughing child, who is now grown;

There's no need to wonder
Which way to go;
No need to wander anymore.

"HIGH" SCHOOL DAYS

[Author's note; the following is a letter from my high school to my mom. Though I don't think I was living at home at the time, I remember intercepting at the mailbox. I was in and out of the house, due to varying levels of altercations with my step-dad at that time who had a bad drinking problem. And my own short fuse and bad temper was admittedly as much to blame as anything. And my mom, (bless you, Mom, you're a saint of a human being, and I love you and owe you so much,) was virtually caught between a rock and a hard place, not really able to intervene.

So that you, reader, may be able to fully appreciate where my head was at in high school, I'll acquaint you with a few important contributing factors. First, I was literally a "straight-A-student" all the way through elementary school. After my First Grade year, I was double-promoted, (against my mom's wishes, it turns out,) to the Third Grade, skipping the Second Grade completely. Though this was a great early scholastic achievement and a mind-blowing honor for me at that very young age, looking back, I honestly would advise a parent against it, and here's why: although I was a 'shining star' in class and always the teacher's pet, I spent those important early formative years with kids who were a year or two older than I was, and therefore more physically and socially developed than I was, meaning they were that degree more mature. I was constantly a target for bullies for years, until I grew big enough and angry enough to hold my own.

The next thing I should point out is, it was the 70's. As a freshman in high school, at twelve years old, I was in advanced classes with juniors and seniors. The older girls all thought I was just the cutest little thing, and therefore all the guys took me under their wing. On rare occasions, I still crossed paths with the more redneck bullies, but for the most part I enjoyed an honorary free pass having so many junior and senior friends. And at that point I discovered several things that I had either not been exposed to before, or that the adults participant in my rearing had tried their best to steer me clear of.

These things were, to wit; Weed, cigarettes, alcohol, the ability to deceive my parents so I could stay out all night and party, that boys will make absolute fools of themselves over girls, and that I was completely bored with school.

Although I didn't believe it was through any personal fault of the teachers, I felt like I was being taught the same thing in school every year, and the things that I felt I really needed to learn to truly understand life and our world were not part of the curriculum.

In those days, in Kentucky, once a kid hit sixteen they could drop out if they chose to. At some point I knew I was just biding my time, waiting for my sixteenth birthday. I was in and out of school as much as I was in and out of the house, eventually ending up at my buddy's inherited farmhouse, and finally, at seventeen, enlisting in the Army as a Cav Scout. I easily got my G.E.D. at the education center at Camp Casey, Republic of Korea.

Anyway, I recently found this letter tucked into an old photo album, and laughed my ass off. I'll insert little explanatory notes throughout to demonstrate why some of the incidents described were funny, in the right context.]

(Centered at the top of the page is the name of my high school, the Principal's name, the school's address, and the date, November 20, 1978.

Below this, aligned left, is my mother's name and address.)
Dear Mrs. Lewis:
This letter is to notify you that Mark is being suspended from school for Tuesday, November 21 and Wednesday, November 22. This action

is necessary because of a fight which Mark had with (another student) in second period study hall, Monday, November 20. The fight was the result of a spitball, name-calling incident which each boy accused the other of starting.

[The other boy and I were actually buddies, and we wanted a couple days off from school. I don't remember which of us actually came up with the idea, but we faked the entire thing, cursing and shoving each other and flinging library books off their shelves, and scaring the hell out of the poor librarian.]

The above incident is just one in a long series of disciplinary problems as noted:

September 28, 1978 - Mark was sent out of fourth period History class for back talk and belligerent attitude-no book and no paper.

[I was probably more bored with History by then than any other class. Same stuff every year, and related from a biased, not necessarily objective perspective, and this particular teacher just gave me too many openings.]

October 3, 1978 – Mark skipped sixth period Agriculture Shop class; didn't let teacher know where he was.

[Ag Shop took up two whole periods and was just too damned easy to skip because it was in a completely separate building, behind the main school and, depending on which door you went out and the time of year it was, any number of unobserved spots presented themselves as possible places to hang out and smoke weed; the branches of the gigantic oak overlooking the baseball field, or the back of the gymnasium, or the boiler room, attached to the side of the Ag Shop building.]

October 4, 1978 – Mark skipped fifth period Agriculture Shop class; was found in library and sent back to class.

[The Ag Shop teacher, who I actually liked, was a tenacious fellow and didn't like it when you skipped his class. He'd set the assistant principal looking for you.]

October 11, 1978 – Mark was found out back of Agriculture building with group of other boys; supposed to be in homeroom or club meeting.

[We had been in the Boiler Room smoking weed, until a lookout spotted the assistant principal approaching and we managed to relocate and head him off before he reached the fog-bank.]

October 12, 1978 – Mark was kissing his girlfriend at the break between second and third periods. One of the faculty members reprimanded him. He paid no attention. When he finished kissing, Mark said to the faculty member, "You'll get over it."

[That's just funny, I don't care who you are.]

October 16, 1978 – Mark said he was sick and needed to go home sixth period. Instead of going home, sat in car on parking lot with two strange fellows.

[This involved drugs. I was sick because I had taken too many pills, and the 'strange fellows' in the parking lot were a couple of friends I'd called who weren't in school to come and pick my ass up. Since it was sixth period anyway, we were waiting for another buddy to get out so he wouldn't have to ride the bus home.]

November 8, 1978 – Mark was sent out of fourth period History class for smart answers and not working.

November 13, 1978 – Mark skipped sixth period agriculture shop class; left school.

November 14, 1978 – skipped second period Study Hall; supposed to go to another room but did not.

[My sixteenth birthday. I dropped out for good soon after.]

As you know, you were sent a letter dated August 4, 1978 explaining that Mark had earned only 7 ½ credits in three years here at the high school. You were also advised that he would only be given a short time to prove that he really did want to pass. Mark has not done this; he failed every subject the first nine weeks grading period of this semester. Mark is currently failing his Agriculture Shop and American History classes; however, he is doing quite well in his Math and English classes. Knowing the ability that Mark has and bearing in mind the disciplinary problems we have with him, it will be absolutely necessary for him to improve for us to allow him to remain in school.

If you would like to talk to us about the above situation, please feel free to call or come to the school.

[It was signed 'Sincerely yours,' by the assistant principal, and had also been forwarded to the office of the county superintendent.]

NOWHERE AVENUE

I find me down at my second home,
Putting a little bleach in my bones,
A quiet harbor from what's out there.

Each drink tastes like the one before,
'Doesn't phase me much anymore,
And it's been awhile since I've seen you around anywhere.

But there's creeps in the dark
And freaks in the park,
All looking for their own kind of score;

And silhouettes in chalk,
Asleep on the sidewalk,
In front of the liquor store
…Down on Nowhere Avenue.

'Call up an old connection,
Trying to beat the resurrection,
But there's no answer, and no sleep again tonight.

And Jesus just hopped a bus for the desert,
'Can't blame him for sitting this one out;
Outside, they've set the tumbleweeds alight.

Now we're all big stars,
Turning over police cars,
That good old 'mob mentality.'

Tear gas from heaven,
'Film at eleven,'
We can go home and watch it on T.V.,
…And wait for the revolution, down on Nowhere Avenue.

Some old beater back-fires outside,
I wonder where you are, and then wonder why,
Sirens cry in the distance.

And I can feel the walls closing in,
As I lie awake and stare at the ceiling,
Trying to remember ever feeling any different.

But the revolution never came, and neither did you,
Everything is just the same, and that's nothing new;
We're all just hanging 'round, waiting for something.

And you can walk but the streets don't won't move,
And no one has heard any news,
Bartender, my friend, keep 'em coming;
…And maybe I'll run into me, down on Nowhere Avenue.

TORTURE IN MOTION

Chasing love,
Man, what was I thinking of?
Always coming back for more;

She'll turn a man to stone,
And say 'Baby, don't you know?
All's fair in love and war.'

Stretched-out there,
On your bed of nails,
A smiling heart attack;

You bring me to the edge
Of sweet oblivion,
Then drag me slowly back.

Now the hour is late,
And a witch's moon hangs in the sky,
'Careful now, don't get burned.

It's alright, just drop that dress,
Beside your high-heeled shoes,
It would seem the game has turned;

Elegant and smooth,
With nothing left to prove,
So refined, you're pure torture in motion.

Finish with me,
And leave me to bleed,
And leave the hemlock potion...I'll drink.

WORLD–WIDE PARTY

I see you there, in the city streets,
Watching as your life rolls by.
There's something missing, you can't hide,
It's all there in your eyes.

I see you, hiding, trembling there in the dark,
Another shadow in another passing night;
Don't run away, don't be afraid anymore,
Take that first step into the sunlight.

I see you there, hanging your head;
I know you're feeling lost, certain you're alone.
Come on in, warm your tired bones,
Come on in, child, out of the cold.

Everybody get up, let's light this fire!
Soon you'll be feeling fine.
Loose your heart's deepest desire,
Come on and take a ride.

It's a Free-Spirit Party,
Come one, baby, come all;
It's a World-Wide Party,
And it's already begun.

'Til The Gods Come Home

(An Historic Prologue:)

[Leap with me mow, reader, 250 years, into an exclusive future which, trust me, we'll explore further together in my literary efforts to come.]

It turns out they really were reverse-engineering extra-terrestrial space craft at Area 51 in Nevada, and the massive underground complex beneath Wright- Patterson Air Base, as well as four other locations around the world. And that scientist who had actually came forward in 1989 claiming to have worked at Area 51, though he'd been discredited and ridiculed at every turn, had been telling the truth.

He claimed these spacecraft operated by means of a gravity wave projection drive system, initiated and sustained through an anti-matter energy reaction which was created by a proton bombardment of an, at that time, undiscovered element. But, despite one hell of a cover-up, once Element 115, Ununpentium, *was* discovered, reproduced in a research lab in 2004, it wouldn't take Mankind long to connect the dots.

And then there had been U.S. President Carlton 'Loose Cannon' Wade. He'd won himself that nickname, and history had honored it ever after. The playing of the supreme high card had been a completely unsanctioned tactic during yet another escalating 'cold war' between world powers. He dropped the ultimate information bomb on not only the American people, but the people of the world.

He announced during a public speech that the U.S. government was in possession of alien space vehicles and, hoping to force the hands of other governments, and in a roundabout way to unite the peoples of the Earth through a common revelation and the necessity of facing up to the implications of that revelation, he demanded his own governmental agencies make such information public and available to the science community at large and demanded the same from other world powers.

There of course was a huge uproar as the conspiracy was revealed in full detail. Years of Congressional hearings and stubborn governmental denial and public outcry ensued. Ultimately, a lot of heads rolled. By the end of his second term in office, there had been three attempts to assassinate President Wade. But the 'Loose Cannon' had come through unscathed.

The weight of the panic and outrage in the streets, combined with a resultant newly-mutated strain of home-grown religious fanaticism, nearly brought the United States to it's knees from within. But, in the end, President Wade's insane gamble won out. America recovered and survived, stronger than ever. Her people had had enough and the face of American politics was changed forever.

The other major global powers began coming clean soon after, under great pressure for reform from their own citizens and key political figures, (who had no doubt realized that President Wade would forever be remembered as a hero.) America had again set the standard. A new era had indeed begun.

The military complexes of the world had in fact secretly been in possession of the spacecraft and physical remains of three distinctive alien races. The only live alien beings ever captured were the two survivors of the crash near Roswell, New Mexico.

The true details of what happened to these aliens still weren't divulged in full for many decades. These beings had been unable, physically, to form any kind of verbal, verbal communication. But their captors quickly realized they were telepathic. And the only thing they seemed to convey through this ability was that they were hostile, angry, and dangerous. It soon became apparent that they were learning how to manipulate human thought and perception.

Unidentified agents from an agency that has also remained unidentified had quickly arrived and responded to the growing crisis at the Roswell Army Air Base by executing the aliens. It seemed a bullet to the brain had the same effect on an alien brain as a human brain.

There were more hearings and more public outcry, but no more heads could be located to offer up to the block. The American military machine subsequently underwent a massive overhaul, combining all branches under one central readiness command, and directly accountable to a Congressional Military Directorate.

Decades before President Wade's shocking revelation, scientists, (notably Stephen Hawking for one,) had theorized that, although it was highly probable that other life had formed and evolved elsewhere in the universe, given the billions of years in which other civilizations could have come and gone, and the vast distances of the cosmos, the odds were pretty slim that we would ever encounter alien races.

Even though it seemed these aliens had beaten those projected odds, science soon realized that in a sense Hawking and the others had been right. When the true potential of the alien technology had been realized, it became clear that they could have come from so far away mankind might never discover their points of origin just by chance.

And it was generally concluded, after what happened with the crash survivors at Roswell, that if we did encounter alien beings, we would likely be completely unable to communicate with them. And given the countenance of the Roswell aliens, would other civilizations have evolved to even understand the concepts of 'peaceful intentions' or 'good-will wishes?'

By 2051, the first test flights buzzed around the inner solar system. In 2054, we went to Proxima Centauri and back, 4.2 light-years away.

But for two-hundred-thirty solar years after President Wade had ushered in his new era, nothing. We did not encounter any other intelligent races.

It was believed the Roswell aliens had come from Zeta Reticuli, a binary star system 39 light-years from Earth in the Reticulum constellation. As a policy of precaution, given their reported demeanor and alleged telepathic abilities, we left them alone, giving their region of space a wide berth.

But, after light-years of exploration, the establishing of numerous colonies and outposts, nothing. We had found numerous moons and planets supporting alien microbial, plant, and animal life, even some primates, but no evidence of any other intelligent beings.

There was, however, the 2012 'Celestial Event,' as history named it, which had never been explained. Nope, our world didn't come to an apocalyptic, cataclysmic ending, as some believed the ancient Mayan Calendar predicted. And there never *was* going to be any 'alignment' of the sun or the solar system or the planets with the 'center' of the galaxy. Because of the actual axis plane of our solar system, and it's position in relation to the equatorial plane in our galaxy, such an alignment had never actually been possible. Yet somehow, through mainstream media, this misinformed belief nonetheless became popular as the date approached.

What *had* happened in 2012 was, on December 2nd of that year, Jupiter, the Earth and the Sun were in alignment. This in itself was not so unusual, as it happens every three-hundred-ninety-nine days, although the latitudinal alignment of Earth and Jupiter was even more precise than what had been calculated and predicted by astronomers, as if some unknown energy or gravitational effect had nudged everything just so.

Many at the time also pointed out that this otherwise commonplace Jupiter Opposition was significant because it coincided with a couple of other important events, one being the eleven year Solar Maximum cycle, a peak in the Sun's magnetic activity. And, the Earth was teetering on the edge of it's twenty-six-thousand year cycle of wobble and tilt on it's axis, which the ancient Mayans, excellent astronomers, had based their calendar on.

'The Celestial Event' itself was what was believed to be the sudden manifestation of some temporary unknown energy/gravitational effect very near to our solar system. Not only did this 'unknown' energy have a noticeable effect on the asteroids out past Pluto, but a very distant comet was observed actually executing an inexplicable course deviation as though some force were tugging at it's orbital path. And accompanying this unknown anomaly was a simultaneous phenomenon that manifested as a great, inexplicable cosmic light show, visible from Earth for exactly twenty-four hours and thirty-seven minutes, in both the day and night sky.

Along the fringe of what appeared as a deeply illuminated dark blue wave in space, outside our solar system, thousands of reddish lights twinkled to life, visible as tiny red X's, twirling and spinning as if alive and intelligent. And over the course of those twenty-four hours, the colors of the twinkling X's and the great wave itself radiated and pulsed in living hues, shifting through spectrums of crimson, blue and violet, all visible from Earth with the naked eye.

But even our most powerful telescopes and brilliant scientists had been unable to explain it. Some had theorized about gamma rays, or the possible visual effects of an unknown alignment of powerful magnetic fields. Other popular rumors and theories of the time suggested alien involvement, but as the 'Celestial Event' occurred almost twenty years before President Wade's incredible announcement, science largely ignored the possibility.

Another pop culture belief that enjoyed prevalence immediately after the fact suggested that all of these coinciding cycles, and the manifestation of the unknown energy phenomenon, and the Jupiter Opposition all combined actually represented a type of space/time map or marker, like coordinates, as a reference point for illuminated beings who had perhaps visited Earth in it's distant past, and had long ago pre-designated those coordinates for a return visit.

In any event, the "Great Light Show of 2012" was never explained, and relatively soon after, Mankind had made it's way to the stars. And for over two centuries, we encountered no one. But in 2263, all of that changed.

'Til The Gods Come Home:
A Science Fiction Novellette

1.

In his office on Orbital Station 129, Lt. Colonel Nathan Landon sipped his morning coffee, taking a seat behind his desk. Having been left on the desk by his secretary, the morning's stack of papers and folders detailed routine reports from the different department heads, both military and civilian, outlining the status of systems functions and internal operations of the evening before.

His personal internal communicator beeped and he picked it up off the desk and flipped it open. "Col. Landon," he acknowledged.

"'Colonel, this is Professor Milifi, in Science."

Of Course Landon knew who the polite old gentleman on the other end was. Milifi was the head of the civilian science department on the orbital station, a very prominent scientist, Rwandan, if he remembered correctly. But the good professor hadn't had reason to call him directly, Landon didn't think, in the fourteen months he'd been in command of the station.

"Good morning, Professor," replied Landon. "How may I be of service to you?"

"I'll try to be brief, 'Colonel. Our instruments are detecting an unusual electro-magnetic disturbance that we are unable to account for."

"I see," said Landon. "Can you localize it? Maybe solar activity or something of that nature?"

"I'm afraid that's where we encounter a bit of a quandary, 'Colonel. While there does seem to be a slight increase in solar activity, it does not seem to be the source of the disturbance. I can find no logical explanation for our readings, and there are some very strong gravitational forces at work that can only originate from some anomaly well outside this small solar system."

"I see," replied Landon. "Could there be any dangerous effects from this...anomaly? To our internal systems, or the outpost on the planet?"

"Perhaps, 'Colonel, if the manifestation intensifies. The station's shielding will protect us from any radiation effects, but we may experience problems with communications, or other similar systems. I have tried to reach Dr. Merriweather on the planet, but have been unable to do so. He has developed some rather intriguing theories in this field. I would very much like to confer with him. I thought perhaps you might be able to establish a more direct link to his remote site."

"I will certainly see what I can do, Professor. Thank you very much for the 'head's up, and please keep me informed of any new developments."

"You are quite welcome, 'Colonel, and I will do so."

Landon closed the channel.

Blowing on the steaming coffee, he turned to the reports again and began thumbing through them. It was way too early for this sort of thing. At least the police blotter was pretty minor. With three-hundred seventy-two people on the station, and all the amenities offered on the Recreation Deck, 'minor' was acceptable. He wondered where Roger was this morning.

Roger Hunt was the Chief of the station's internal civilian police force. On most mornings he would have been in Landon's office by now, comparing notes about the evening watch reports or coordinating for any important activities of the day, and relating the newest dirty joke he may have heard. About the time he noticed the pink file in the stack, the color code indicating a low order abnormality, was the same moment his friend Roger entered his office through the open door with Captain Martina Hernandez in tow. Landon pulled the pink file. Sure enough it was from Communications, Captain Hernandez's department. He opened the file and began skimming over it.

"' Morning, Nate," Roger Hunt greeted him. He always seemed to especially enjoy being aloof and informal with his friend in the presence of other military personnel.

"Roger," Landon acknowledged him without looking up from the report. Hunt had parked himself on a corner of the large desktop.

"Captain Hernandez reporting, sir." When any anomalous report went to the Station Commander, it was protocol for the head of that department or a representative to report to the Commander's office to brief him on the details.

Landon looked up at her. She was a Latin beauty, mid-thirties, deep brown eyes and long jet-black hair which she always wore pinned up in the back and tucked under her blue Signal Corps beret when she was on duty. And the way she filled out her Military Readiness Command ("Mirc" or "Mircom") coveralls was distracting, to say the least. Landon always had to make an actual effort to maintain his professional demeanor when he encountered her.

"Please, Captain, be at ease," he said, smiling, gesturing to a chair opposite the desk from him. "Take a seat if you'd like. 'Commo problems last night?" he asked, looking back down at the report.

"Yes, sir," she replied. "When I relieved Lieutenant Chan this morning on watch, he informed me that an anomalous increase in, what seemed like electro-magnetic activity, was causing some unusual interference with the communications systems."

Landon sensed a little uncertainty from her. Something in her tone said she wished she could be more specific. "'What *seemed* like electro-magnetic activity?" he back-tracked for her.

She seemed a little uneasy for a moment, hesitant to offer anything more if she didn't believe it to be more definitive. "Well, sir, while the intermittent interference has the characteristic symptoms of a typical electro-magnetic disturbance, it also displays symptoms that aren't so typical. Characteristics we're unable to explain."

"I just received a call from Professor Milifi in civilian science. He said just about the same thing," said Landon. "Are internal communication systems affected?"

"No, sir," Hernandez replied. "Only the external push and the carrier wave radio systems."

"Are we still receiving the transponder signals from stations 97 and 132?"

"Yes, sir," she said, "and last night's watch was able to establish direct contact with them. They confirmed the same disturbance is detectable in their areas as well."

Landon stood now and moved to the large portal window, looking down at the planet below, which the station orbited. The captivating, small, green and blue world, NY-494-Alpha, revolved ever so slowly beneath them. "What about the science station?" he asked.

"The transponder and direct communications are still functional at this time, sir," Hernandez replied.

Landon visually surveyed the region of space beyond the portal. The small star and the two planets of this system were in the neighborhood of Spica, in the constellation Virgo. The only station further out in space was 132.

"Captain, I'd like you to get with Lt. Miller in Long Range Observation. See if he can use the Mirc optics to look for whatever's kicking up all the dust. And see if you can speak with Professor Milifi. He might be able to offer some assistance. I'm going to go to ops and see if I can contact Dr. Merriweather down on the planet and see if he has any ideas."

She agreed and he dismissed her. But just before Captain Hernandez turned to go, Landon could have sworn he caught just the hint of a smile, slight dimples appearing just at the corners of her mouth. Perhaps he was just imagining it, but it was if she sensed his attraction to her, and allowed him his flattering efforts.

"I saw that," Roger chided him, after she had gone, still seated on the corner of his desk.

"Saw what?" Landon returned his aloofness now.

"You know damned well what."

"What do you know about the good Captain?" He had been single for a few years now, since his wife, Elaine, had divorced him. She hadn't been able to wait out the long haul with only brief visits once or twice a year.

"I know she's incredibly hot," Roger commented.

That she was, Landon nodded. Perhaps he should get back in the game.

"And I know she's very single," Roger added.

"Are you sure?" Landon was surprised. Okay, maybe he'd play along with Roger. It was pleasant to think about anyway. And as sore and withdrawn as he'd been since the divorce, maybe a good 'chase' was just what he needed.

"Nate," Roger was taken aback. "I'm *'the cops'*, I know everything about everybody, even your people."

"She's way too fantastic. How could she be…romantically uninvolved? Mircom officers are usually very discreet about fraternization, as an informal policy anyhow. Perhaps no one knows about it."

"Amigo," Roger stood now, his arms out, palms up. "I'm your buddy. I would not steer you wrong."

"Yeah, you're my buddy alright. Enough of a buddy to laugh your ass off when I make a fool of myself."

Roger put a hand on his shoulder. "Of course," he smiled, "that's what buddies are for."

Landon chuckled. "You asshole. 'Want to go to ops with me?"

"Sure, what the hell?" Roger rarely had anything pressing. They left the office and headed down the corridor together.

"So what do you make of this…what did she call it? Electro-magnetic disturbance? I noticed it was only in a pink folder, so I'm guessing it's not *that* big of a deal."

Landon turned to smirk at him. "Not yet anyway."

For the first time that morning Roger Hunt's ever-present smile took brief pause, nearing reservation, even, Landon assessed. He'd gotten him.

"'Could be nothing," Landon said. "A solar flare from a nearby star, maybe, more intense than we're used to seeing. Or an unusually large rogue asteroid or something passing through the neighborhood. Hell, I don't know, I'm not a 'renowned physicist.'"

Roger's smile returned now. "But, it just so happens, you know where to find one."

That was the good thing about Roger, he could usually find his own way to your point. Doctor Miles Merriweather was heralded far and wide as one of Science's most brilliant minds, and this *wunderkinder* was on the surface of the planet below, a member of the research team at the science station. He had apparently developed a fascination with a particular geological site discovered near the station and had been on the planet for four months. Landon had met him a couple of times. He seemed like an affable fellow, younger than he'd expected.

In a few moments they'd reached 'ops,' the operational nerve center and central command for Orbital Station 129 and all her tech and logistics systems. The command center was abuzz with activity this morning. There were more personnel present than usual, accompanying several department head officers who normally rarely had reason to appear in ops. Several diagnostic programs appeared to be running at various main systems stations.

"'Busy place," remarked Roger.

"Yeah," confirmed Landon, a little suspiciously, "it is."

They were greeted by Major Ellsworth, Landon's executive officer, second in command of the military branch of the station's infrastructure. "Good morning, 'Colonel." He turned to Roger, with a nod. "Chief Hunt."

"Hi, Bob," said Landon. "What's all the hubbub?"

"Well, sir, in about the last half-hour several departments have began reporting various systems fluctuations and abnormalities. We're running diagnostics protocols now."

Landon turned to shoot Roger a curious glance. Again, Roger Hunt's smile checked itself.

Landon approached the carrier wave radio alcove, manned by a young black warrant officer. "Mr. Preston, will you establish a channel with the science station, please? See if they can connect me with Dr. Merriweather."

"Yes, sir." Mr. Preston activated his console.

Landon turned back to Roger and Bob Ellsworth, who had been casually trailing him. "'Heard anything from L.R.O.?" he asked the Major.

"No, sir, Long Range Observation hasn't contacted me this morning."

Landon voice-activated his hand-held internal communications device, which would in turn contact the appropriate station or individual. "'Colonel Landon to L.R.O."

"This is Lt. Miller, sir," came a quick enough response.

"Good morning, Lieutenant. Listen, we're getting a lot of systems interference that seems electro-magnetic in nature. Have you guys noticed anything on your optics or sensor probe relays that could account for the disturbance?"

"I've just been talking with Captain Hernandez about that, sir. We haven't detected anything unusual on optics. But the probe relays seem to be...malfunctioning."

"'Malfunctioning' how?" Landon prompted him.

"They seem to be transmitting faulty data."

Landon pondered this for a moment. "Or," he said then, "the sensor probes themselves could be malfunctioning."

"Possibly, sir," replied Miller.

"And what kind of faulty data are we talking here, Miller?"

"Well sir, the readings would seem to indicate a localized ...increase.. in the established levels of background radiation."

Landon shook his head. He didn't like the turn this morning was taking. Science wasn't really his specialty so he wasn't exactly clear on why Miller doubted the accuracy of the sensor probe telemetry.

"Right," he finally responded. "Lieutenant, activate all optical observation banks and long range sensor instruments, and initiate a full 'alert' level sweep. And get some techs working on the sensor probe problem. Keep me apprised of any developments. Landon out."

Mr. Preston called to him now. "Sir, I have the science station. Dr. Merriweather is out in the field and they can't establish communication with his team at this time."

"Is Lt. Jones available?" Landon asked. Jones was the commander of the M.R.C. Security detachment at the science station.

"Yes, sir, he's actually in the commo shack," replied Preston.

Landon moved over to the console. "Lt. Jones, can you hear me? It's 'Colonel Landon."

"Loud and clear for the moment, sir," came a response.

"Do you have a relay fix on the coordinates of Dr. Merriweather's team?"

"Yes, sir," Jones answered from the surface. "I know exactly where they are."

"Lieutenant, I want you to send a team out to try and re-establish communication with Dr. Merriweather. I need to speak with him."

"Will do, sir."

Landon's internal communicator beeped again. "L.R.O. to 'Colonel Landon."

He and Ellsworth shot each other a surprised glance. "That was fast," said Roger.

"Landon here."

"Miller, sir. We just observed a pretty intense solar flare. Professor Milifi is here now, and I have to agree with his conclusion that, while a flare will add to the interference, in this case it's just another symptom of the main disturbance, which is outside this system."

"That would have to be one hell of a disturbance," Ellsworth said.

From the main communication center, Preston called over his shoulder again. "'Colonel, I just got a weak message from the science station. They confirm their instruments show a sudden increase in solar activity as well."

"Is their signal degrading?" Landon asked him.

"There is an increase in interference, sir, but their signal does seem to be steady at the moment."

"Mr. Preston, please advise the science station to be prepared to go to a pulsed signal if we lose communication."

"'Think anyone in the commo shack knows how to operate the pulsed system?" Roger asked him.

Landon could only shrug. The pulsed signal system was kind of an advanced take on the old Morse Code, a backup system in place in case of a communication failure. Over a short distance, like a planet's surface to an orbital station, the antiquated system could usually get a signal through the interference of even a severe electro-magnetic disturbance. But it was rarely ever necessary to use it.

Landon turned to Major Ellsworth. "Isn't there a Cruiser Group nearby?"

"The U.S.S. King Group is two sectors away on maneuvers. That's probably twenty-two hours at best speed," he replied.

"Let's try and raise them on carrier wave and advise them of our situation."

"Yes, sir."

As the Major strode away, Roger Hunt eyed his friend. "A cruiser group?"

Landon offered a reassuring smile. "Better to have and not need, than to need and not have."

2.

On the planet's surface, in the commo shack, 'Scotty' Price, the civilian communications operator at the science station sat back heavily against the back of his chair and stroked his shortly-groomed beard. 'Pulsed signal?' He eyed the dormant apparatus to his right, taking up that entire end of the building.

"Damn, really?" he grumbled under his breath. He knew where the manual was for the code itself, although he'd be excruciatingly slow at best. But the thing probably hadn't been switched on since the station was built seven years before. He supposed they probably should have been conducting periodic tests on the system to insure it would even function if they ever needed it.

He turned to his left. On the other side of the front door, two of the station's scientists were puzzling over instrumentation monitors, about some nonsensical data relayed from the distant deep space sensor probes on station well outside this small solar system.

"Hey, Shim, ever operate a pulsed signal generator?" Scotty called over to one of the researchers.

"Not me, brother. I'm not going anywhere near that thing," replied the young Korean man. "You're the 'commo guy.'"

"Julie, sweetie," he focused his charm on the other researcher, a young blonde woman. "I know how you love a good challenge."

She laughed at him. "A good chess game, or downing shots of tequila, maybe. A radioactive death trap? Not going to happen…'sweetie.'"

"You should try one of the Mircom guys," Shim said.

Scotty's eyes widened. Great idea. He sprang out of his chair, towards the open metal door. "Crap," he said, remembering something, then turning and dashing back for his station. He grabbed the remote headset and slipped it on over his backwards cap and headed for the door again.

"Ooh," he stopped again in the doorway, remembering something else. "Julie, I actually happen to know where I can get my hands on a bottle of tequila…'sweetie.'"

"You'd better catch them, I think they're leaving," Julie Burlington urged him.

He shot her his handsome grin and headed out the door and down the steps. Lt. Jones was just passing by with three other soldiers. He hurried to come alongside them. "Lt. Jones, how's your Morse code?"

Jones turned to acknowledge him, but kept walking. They were headed for the motor pool, and Scotty noticed they were armed.

The Lieutenant understood that 'Col. Landon must have been concerned about a loss of communications. "Go check the barracks," he said. "Find Sergeant Hackett, he's operated a pulse generator before. Tell him I said to standby at the commo shack in case you need him."

"Thanks, Lieutenant," said Scotty, relieved. Then, out of curiosity he asked, "So…what's with the hardware?"

Specialist 4th Class Noel Bailey answered with a chuckle, stroking the light machinegun hanging from his shoulder by it's sling. "Better to have and not need than the other way 'round," he said in his Arkansas accent.

Scotty froze in his tracks as the soldiers kept walking. Surely they weren't worried about the sonic emitters going down, too. That could be bad, really bad. He eyed the dense jungle outside the compound fence. This planet was home to a variety of different species of wildlife, some very dangerous, even predatory. And the only thing keeping them from wandering into the camp was the sophisticated sonic emitter network in place around the perimeter and along the main roads and trails that had been cut. He turned now and jogged off toward the cluster of three long gray metal barracks buildings housing the Military Readiness Command personnel.

Eleven kilometers from the science station, beneath a canvas-roofed shelter, a large tent with the sides rolled up, Miles Merriweather stood at a long portable lab table littered with instruments, tools, samples, and beakers. He stooped slightly, peering into a microscope at the results of his latest reactive test on some stone samples. Again, negative results.

"Damn," he murmurs under his breath. Something long ago had altered the molecular structure of the stone deposits in the ground here in this vast open plane. But this oddity was found nowhere else on the planet, only this particular savannah. While he still wasn't sure what had caused the transformation, he was getting closer to ruling out all the things that hadn't.

"There's not much else left," he said to himself.

"Are you talking to yourself again, Miles?" One of his colleagues strolled beneath the canvas, a taller, shirtless, English fellow in knee-length utility trousers, named Charles Pearson. "I keep telling everyone you're perfectly mad, you know."

Merriweather looked up at him, grinning. "Charlie, you know I'm right about this place."

"And you know I'm right about you. Perfectly mad." Pearson was several years the senior scientist, but he had a great deal of respect for 'the wiz kid,' and he knew that Miles appreciated his light cajoling and candor. "Are you going to come have some dinner with the rest of us?"

Miles glanced over at the palatial bus. "How long do you plan on parking that eyesore on my site?"

"Miles, dear boy, we've all the comforts of home only a few meters away, although Natalie says the bloody commo is down again. Come on, have a meal."

Merriweather knew Pearson wouldn't take 'no' for an answer. And he *was* a little hungry now that he thought about it. But before he turned to follow, he glanced once more at the bright sky of this tiny tropical world. A brilliant light had crept over the horizon, opposite the low sitting sun behind him, the system's only other planet, the massive gas giant on the outer rim.

3.

Two soldiers closed the high steel mesh gate behind Lt. Jones' rover as they departed the compound, a sergeant named Norwood behind the wheel. Directly in front of them the first of many sonic emitter monitors shone a steady green light. Norwood shifted aggressively into third gear and the lightly armored four-wheeled truck sped by it.

Lt. Jones sat in the front passenger seat, a map tucked loosely in a console rack beside him. But they had been out to where Dr. Merriweather spent most of his time on a regular basis, and this main road led straight to it. Eleven kilometers, no sweat, they'd be there in about half an hour.

Jones turned to the two Spec. 4's in the open cargo area in the back. 'Noel Bailey from Arkansas' was standing up, braced against a corner behind the vehicle's crew-served weapon, a Russian-made 8.22 millimeter machinegun. Jones smiled. He knew the kid was eating this up. On a low bench seat opposite him, Lopez , the other enlisted man was assembling some radio components on the floor.

Jones knew the little Puerto Rican knew his stuff, but gave him a little start anyway. "Lopez, goddammit, did you check that shit before we left?"

"You know I did, sir," Lopez replied without looking up.

"Are you getting smart with me, Specialist?"

Lopez looked up now with a smile. "Oh hell no, sir."

"Outstanding," responded Jones.

The rover hooked the road's first bend and the jungle closed behind them to swallow the outpost. The Lieutenant flipped on the rover's external push radio mounted on the broad dashboard and attempted to establish contact with his command post at the station.

"Mircom X-ray 7, this is 7 Rover 5, radio check, over."

"This is X-ray 7, roger." The signal had some static but seemed strong enough.

Jones eyed the jungle ahead as it nudged up to each side of the dusty road. Around the next bend, still in the distance, he knew they'd pass the next sonic emitter monitor. That would mark the first kilometer.

He sat quietly as they drove on, listening to banter between Norwood and Bailey. Soon enough, Lopez seemed satisfied his equipment was ready to be installed when they reached the remote site, and he joined in the joking between the others. They rounded the next bend and Jones could see the bright green light ahead. Smooth sailing.

They drove on for a few kilometers, each marked by the green monitor lights. They passed a fork in the road and a couple of roads leading away in either direction, and the jungle every so often receded to reveal grassy planes. One such open area even accessed a lake a few hundred meters away.

The soldiers talked and joked about the things soldiers will talk and joke about. Soon, in the distance ahead, Lt. Jones could just discern the crossroads he was waiting for. From there they would be in sight of the ninth emitter monitor.

As they approached the crossroads, the rover's radio crackled, the static very intense now. Jones just made out the command post call-sign, but the rest was so distorted he couldn't decipher it.

"What the hell?" he muttered, leaning closer to the radio. He pressed the side of his remote headset. "X-ray 7, this is 7 Rover 5, please say again, your signal is distorted and unreadable, over."

There was another attempt from the command post, this time even more distorted. Lt. Jones turned to Bailey, still standing in the back. "Unclip that antenna."

Bailey reached over and unhooked the tie-down clip holding the sturdy whip aerial pulled back horizontally. It sprang upward, swaying back and forth.

Jones tried the radio again. "X-ray 7, 7 Rover 5, please respond, over." The radio remained ominously silent now.

Suddenly, Norwood began to slow the vehicle. Jones looked up at him curiously, not liking what he saw in Norwood's expression. Then he saw the fearful look in Lopez's eyes as he leaned forward from the back to peer through the windshield.

"Oh, shit," Jones heard Bailey say behind him.

He turned back forward just as Norwood pulled the rover to a stop in the center of the crossroads. Ahead in the distance, they were indeed within sight of the ninth monitor. The bright light shone a deep red warning. The sonic emitter system which kept the indigenous wildlife at a safe distance was down.

Their jaws all dropped, they only had a split-second to register this development. Bailey caught a blurred movement out of the corner of his eye and turned. His heart stopped in his chest. Something big was upon them.

He tried too late to alert Norwood behind the wheel. "GO! GO! GO!"

A monstrous, huge shape moving at a high velocity rammed the rover broadside and rolled it over in the intersection of the crossroads. Jones suddenly realized he was on his back on the dry dirt road, looking up at the rover's floor plate. The open-roofed vehicle was upside-down, but held suspended above him by a bent support strut. He was choking on the thick dust.

"It's coming back," he could hear Bailey screaming. Then another sound. A machinegun bolt chambering live ammunition.

Lopez was crawling in through the open, mangled passenger side door. Bailey opened fire on something, shouting to him. "You gotta get him out! I don't think I can stop it!"

"I've got you, L.T.," Lopez was saying. He had Jones by his coveralls, dragging him out. "Push with your feet, man!"

They were both out from under it now. Bailey had stopped firing and was dashing for the jungle. On his heels, a great pachyderm beast galloped after him, bellowing furiously. The animal closely resembled an Earth rhinoceros, though it's size was closer to a small elephant's. Instead of any horns or protrusions, it's massive forehead was a broad, flat sort of raised rectangular lobe above it's angry eyes and dark beak-like snout. It had made to charge the rover again, but Bailey, having been thrown clear like Lopez had, managed to distract the beast. But the light weapon had only enraged the beast more and it now was after him full-bore.

Bailey made it safely into the dense jungle, hurtling into the harsh undergrowth. The beast halted at the edge of the jungle. It was large and needed room to maneuver, preferring this open intersection to the tight confines of the jungle brush. Forty or fifty meters away now, it swung it's massive head back around to eyeball Lopez and Jones.

The beast's body seemed almost to pivot on an axis to align behind it's battering ram head. It meant to charge something. Lt. Jones scanned the intersection, still dazed. Where was Norwood?

"L.T., we gotta move!" Lopez was charging his weapon, preparing to fire at the beast, which was now in full gallop again, coming at them.

Jones looked at the ruined rover. There it was, the big Russian 8.22. The smaller personal weapons didn't seem to affect the animal, but surely the big machinegun would. The weapon had been torn loose from it's mount, but lay alongside the rover on the dirt road. The cartridge belts, however, were inside the vehicle, folded into ammo cans. He'd have to go back under it. But the massive animal was getting closer.

Lopez opened fire as Jones still crouched beside the smashed rover. "Lopez! See if you can draw it away!"

That plan was already in action. Lopez was running for the safety of the dense jungle, turning to fire short bursts at the thing on the fly. The beast veered away from the rover and after him.

Lt. Jones was back under the rover. He spotted the ammo cans, strapped to a rack on the wall. But he also saw something else. Through the bent driver's-side door, he spotted a twisted heap that he knew was Sgt. Norwood, lying unmoving just on the other side of the rover. He looked like the rover had rolled over on him.

Jones rolled onto his back and slid back underneath the cargo area. The weight of the ammo cans had the strap in a bind and he couldn't unhook it. *Not a problem.* He produced a large knife from it's station on his utility vest and began sawing at the sturdy strap. Somewhere outside, he heard Bailey calling to Lopez.

"Stay in the jungle! Move to your right so I can fire!"

The freed ammo cans tumbled down on him, even though he'd tried to move out of the way. One put a nasty gash on his forehead. He tried to shake it off as he heard Bailey open fire on the beast. More enraged bellowing. Jones heard the animal gallop past again, headed the other direction. He crawled out with a cartridge belt just in time to see Bailey bounding back into the jungle as the beast pulled up short again.

He had the big weapon in his hands now, kicking the tripod legs down as he sat on his behind. The massive, bulldozer-like pachyderm had turned again, eyeing him now as he fumbled with the feed tray cover. The animal charged.

The belt's end cartridge in place, Jones slammed the cover shut and pulled the charging handle. The beast was bearing down on him at a full run. Bracing his boots against the tripod legs, he squeezed the trigger. The weapon began barking loudly, spewing smoke and bullets, lurching against his shoulder.

Jones could see the rounds impacting the creature, and he wondered for a moment whether the creature would drop before it crushed him against the overturned rover. But suddenly the juggernaut lurched, wavering oddly, then standing upright on it's rear legs, bellowing angrily. The animal's belly exposed to him now, he maintained his fire. He could see the big 8.22 rounds splaying the beast open and chewing it's innards.

With a final roar, the beast convulsed, then teetered, still on it's hind legs, and finally collapsed before him. Less than fifteen feet in front of him, the monster's massive ribs expanded, then released it's final breath. Jones released the trigger and the machinegun fell silent. Still shaking, he sat the butt of the weapon down in the dust, it's muzzle end still smoldering. He flipped the selector to 'safe.'

Bailey came running up now and stood beside the felled behemoth, dumbfounded, shaking from his own adrenaline surge. "What the hell *is* that thing?"

Steadying himself against the smashed rover, Jones pulled himself to his feet. He heard Lopez cursing on the other side of the vehicle.

Running around to that side, Jones now saw the extent of Norwood's condition. The rover had crushed him when it rolled. "He's dead," Lopez confirmed.

Jones was trying to fight off the state of shock that was trying to catch up with him. This had all happened way too fast. And he and Norwood had been good friends. What the hell was going on? An image of Norwood smiling over a good Poker hand flashed in his head.

"L.T., we've got to get back to the station." Bailey was alongside him now.

"If the sonics are down we are way beyond screwed, man." Lopez was ready to leave.

"See if you can find a tarp or something to cover him with," said Jones. Lopez began prying open a utility compartment.

Jones turned to Bailey. "We're a lot closer to Merriweather's site than we are to the station."

"But, L.T., with the sonics down everybody out there might already be dead," said the young soldier.

"That could be, but there's at least two vehicles out there," said Jones. He knew, besides that huge bus, there was a civilian rover out there. Lopez unfolded a canvas tarp and covered Norwood's body.

"Alright, listen up." The Lieutenant's command instincts were taking over. "We're about eight-and-a-half kilometers from the station, so that means it's about two- and-a-half to the site. And we've got about three to four hours of daylight left. Bring water and ammunition. And crack open that case of grenades. Each of us will carry four. So, let's get moving. It's time to earn our pay."

They hastily gathered up their gear. As they moved out on foot, Bailey stood alongside the sprawled beast for one last look at it.

Lopez called to him. "Come on, man. That thing's dead."

"It's not him I'm worried about," said Bailey.

4.

At the site, the handful of unwary scientists and techs sat in the dining area of the big bus. Dinner was lasagna and garlic bread from the freezer. Professor Pearson had donned a T-shirt for the meal and was continuing his banter with Merriweather as the others enjoyed their food.

"So, Miles, anything new from all those tests?" Pearson asked, adding a slight chuckle.

"Well, Charlie, all I can say is, every time I can eliminate a possibility, I'm that much closer to finding what I'm looking for," replied Merriweather.

One of the other scientists joined in now, an older French woman, a geologist named Dori Prideux. "So, Miles, you still do not believe the transformation of these deposits at a molecular level occurred naturally?"

Miles turned to her. "Do you, Dori? You've examined the rock yourself. And why only here? In this almost perfectly square plane, which just happens to be very close to the dimensions of the base of the Great Pyramid of Giza, and the Pyramid of the Sun at Teotihuacan?"

Dori smiled warmly. "I agree that this planet offers no clues to the mysterious metamorphosis of these deposits. But it is quite a scientific leap to connect the dimensions of this plane to those of ancient structures on Earth. You said yourself, the dimensions are very close, but not exact. Even the two pyramids you mention are not exactly the same."

"True," conceded Merriweather, "but there are other striking similarities. And what about the site on Mars? Same shape and roughly the same dimensions."

Dori smiled kindly. "But Miles, your Martian site is little more than a rock-strewn plane."

"Ah," he continued. "But the rocks are the same as here, altered at the molecular level."

"Oui," agreed Dori, "I'll grant you this. But still this is not definitive proof of a physical connection."

Before Merriweather could continue, a technician named Natalie Plant entered the dining area, seemingly disgusted. "I don't know what's wrong with the radio," she sighed, throwing her hands in the air.

Another tech, a Dutchman named Thedo Vandenhoek, suddenly leaped from his chair, stammering, frowning intently at something through the big window. "What the hell?"

The seven others seated at the table turned to look. Something glanced against the side of the bus, a reddish-brown blur streaking past the bottom of the window. All their faces went slack. Across the wide plane, a large herd of deer or antelope-like creatures were bounding past. And that only meant one thing.

"The sonics are down," said Merriweather, his voice calm and even. Three months ago, he had helped techs install the system around the perimeter of this place and connect it to the main system. The sonic emitter system normally created a directed and sustained vibrational field at a frequency intolerable to most animal and even insect life, and would keep them at least a hundred meters from a linear perimeter, like those around the science station and along the roads and trails. But it had to be functional first.

Another animal banged against the side of the bus. Merriweather's thoughts flashed on his open air tent outside. "My lab!"

He made to dash out but Pearson grabbed his shoulder. "Wait!"

Merriweather turned back to the window amid gasps from the others. A huge cougar-like animal had just tackled a straggling antelope and now rolled with it in the dust as it struggled. Two more of the enormous cats flew by at incredible speeds.

"Are there any guns on this bus?" Merriweather asked.

"Those, we have," said Vandenhoek.

At the science station, Scotty Price sat in the cafeteria, eating a cheeseburger. He still had his remote headset on, though the little bit of communication traffic he'd had with the orbital station was growing weaker and weaker. But, not to worry, Sgt. Hackett assured him he'd hang out at the commo shack, ready to fire up the pulse generator in case regular communication channels failed.

The twenty or so other diners around him in the cafeteria were quite a diverse variety. There were Mircom personnel, in their coveralls and berets, as well as researchers and techs, dressed in everything from lab coats to denim bib overalls. His friends, Julie Burlington and Bong-hwa Shim, entered now through the open door.

Scotty gave them a wave and they nodded, smiling, moving toward the tray stacks. He knew they'd get their chow and come sit with him. He swatted at a fly that buzzed by him. Then he realized what that meant. He leaped from his bench and ran to the door.

He heard the alarmed shout from the operations building at the same time he saw the glaring red light just beyond the mesh gate. "The sonics are down!" someone shouted. A loud alert horn let out three ear-splitting blasts. People began filing out of the structures around the camp, looking at the red signal of the sonic emitter monitor.

As Scotty stepped out in front of the cafeteria with some of the other personnel, in his headphones he heard two sets of three quick beeps. "Shit," he muttered to those beside him. "Commo's completely out, too."

He was about to turn and head for the commo shack when a woman behind him said, "Look!" she was pointing at something outside the fence.

When he heard the sharply-drawn breath around him, he stopped to look as well. Two big cats were prowling around in the cleared buffer zone beyond the fence. Scotty remembered this species from the orientation film. They looked like steroid-enhanced mutations of pumas, but nearly twice the size. And the fur behind their necks and jaws was fuller, bushier, similar to a lion's mane, but with a much different placement and profile.

He realized that if one of those things figured out it could clear the fence, it would probably make a quick meal of the first person it could get it's paws on. Just then, a good-sized monkey made the mistake of wandering into the buffer zone. The cats sprang into a run and chased after the animal, pursuing it back into the jungle.

"They'll come back," someone said. Scotty took off for the commo shack.

The senior enlisted man under Lt. Jones was a Filipino Sergeant First Class named Ralphriel Abaya, and he now approached with a bullhorn loudspeaker device. "Okay, people, you know the protocol, everyone get indoors and stay there until this is over. All Mircom personnel report to the Arms Room and draw personal and crew-served weapons."

Scotty hopped up the steps and into the commo shack. Sgt. Hackett had the pulse generator console lit up. The apparatus hummed to life.

"Well, I can see you're right on top of things, Sarge," Scotty said. "Is the thing going to work?"

"It's receiving okay," said Hackett. "I just got a signal from orbital, asking for a response. Hang on." He opened the transmitter box and tapped code over the keying device.

"Did you tell them the sonics are down?" Scotty asked him.

"Yeah," replied Hackett. "Hang on." He raised a pencil off the console and readied a pad of paper. A series of long and short beeps from a speaker followed as Sgt. Hackett transcribed. The response translated as *'Standby. Follow protocols. Troubleshoot, identify problem, attempt repair. Standby.'*

"Hey, do me a favor will you?" Hackett asked Scotty.

"Whatever you need, Sarge."

"Grab one of my guys outside and tell them to bring me my weapons. Tell them I can't leave the commo shack."

Scotty eyed him coolly. "Better to have and not need, eh, Sarge?" He truly felt at ease now with the well-known, unofficial slogan of the Military Readiness Command. Now he understood.

"Damned straight," Hackett smiled at him. "And I'll tell you something else. There's more going on here than just some fucking solar flares. All those lab coats that have been in and out of here, debating and scratching their heads over their instrument readings over there, they're pretty spooked. There's something going down in this a.o. that they can't explain."

Scotty felt goose-bumps raise on his arms. "Thanks. Now I'm spooked, too," he said as he turned to go.

5.

On Orbital Station 129, Lt. Col. Landon sat in the Mircom cafeteria with Roger Hunt. "Take me with you," Roger said. Landon was taking a shuttle to the surface as soon as he finished his meal.

"But, Roger, we're not sure what effect this disturbance is having on their systems down there," Landon said, attempting to discourage his friend.

"I want to go," Roger feigned a whiny voice.

"What if their sonic emitters are down?"

"Nate, I've seen the orientation films! I get it! There's 'lions, and tigers, and bears, oh, no!' I've got a gun."

"You're sure?" asked Landon, prepared to give in.

"Nate, I haven't been off this station in three months. I need some fresh air. Besides, there's what, an entire Mircom Rifle Company down there? I'm in good hands, right? I'm not worried."

"Okay," Landon said. "You can go." His com device beeped and he flipped it open. "Landon," he answered.

"'Colonel Landon, this is Professor Milifi. I understand you are taking a shuttle to the planet's surface."

"Yes, Professor I am," he replied.

"I was wondering if I might go down with you. It is very important that I speak with Dr. Merriweather."

Landon paused, glaring at Roger. "'See what you started?"

"What's that, 'Colonel?" Milifi asked.

"I'm sorry, Professor, I was speaking to someone else. Can you be on the hangar deck in twenty minutes?"

"I'll be there. Good-bye, 'Colonel.'"

"Good-bye," replied Landon, terminating the connection.

A growing murmur and several other cafeteria patrons turning in their chairs caught Roger's attention, so he turned to the huge view port as well. Then he and Landon were both slowly taking their feet.

As everyone watched, aghast, a distant sector of space began to light up, a faint, bluish glow at first, then a quick, fiery, orange-red flash as the phenomenon burst into existence along a defined fringe that looked as separate from space as a gigantic blanket might, floating on a steady wind, and at the same time resembling a long rip in a huge sail.

The initial fiery flash subsided, and the rip began to glow warmly, deep blue and crimson shades seeming to roil forth now within. And as the phenomenon grew and it's edges spread out, the space within it's inner maw blackened, thickening somehow. No stars were visible behind it.

Landon's communication device beeped. "L.R.O. to 'Colonel Landon.'"

"Yeah, I see it, Miller," Landon responded. "What the hell is it?"

"I've never seen anything like it, sir," replied Lt. Miller. "Professor Milifi is still here. He's also at a loss."

"Right," said Landon. "Tell the Professor if he still wants to go to the surface let's get a move on. Landon out." He snapped the device shut. "Hurry up and eat, Roger. I'll leave you."

Landon picked up his tray and walked away, leaving his friend hurriedly cramming food in his mouth. The one man who might know what was going on was down on the surface. The quicker he found Dr. Merriweather the better.

Fifteen minutes later, Landon was at the back door of the shuttle, looking over the maintenance tech's pre-flight checklist as three armed enlisted men stood by, along with a flight systems tech officer. The shuttle could seat ten, plus the pilot. The enlisted men were assigned to Landon as personal security by the Executive Officer, Major Ellsworth. The flight tech who would be accompanying them was a Warrant Officer named Carter Willis.

Landon checked his watch, looking around. Just then Roger Hunt came sprinting onto the hangar deck, a light pack on his shoulder and a pump shotgun in his hand. As he reached the back of the shuttle, Landon asked him, "What are you going to do with that?"

"I'm a cop, I can have a gun," Roger replied. Nodding at the security detail, he added, "*they* have guns."

"I wonder where Milifi is," said Landon.

"Sir?" called a female voice. They turned to see Captain Martina Hernandez approaching. Caught off guard, Landon's heart skipped a beat. He knew then that his attraction for her had perhaps become something more over the past few months after all.

"Permission to accompany the landing party to the surface, sir?" she asked.

Curious and a little amazed, Landon asked, "Why?"

Now she was off guard. She obviously hadn't expected him to be hesitant. She stammered only slightly before forming an answer. "I may be able to help with their communications problem, sir, or at least gain a new insight into the nature of the disturbance."

He smiled warmly. It was feeble reasoning at best, full of holes he could have pointed out. But he decided to let things play out. And he knew that a deeper part of him he didn't want to acknowledge wanted her with him. Something very weird was unfolding here, and if things got dangerous, he could protect her. "Captain, it would be an honor to have you on our landing party. Welcome aboard."

With a semi-smile that lingered somewhere between affection and flirtation, she thanked him and climbed into the shuttle to take a seat. Landon turned to the others. "Go ahead and get on board, gentlemen. We'll give the professor five minutes."

Roger Hunt lingered outside the craft with him, waiting for the others to be out of earshot. "You old dog. No wonder you didn't want me along."

"What?" snapped Landon. "I didn't know she was coming!"

"Whatever, Slick," Roger chuckled at him. "Man, you work fast. What is it, some kind of mind control? Hypnosis? You've got to teach me."

"Will you knock it off?" Landon berated him.

"Okay, okay," Roger laughed. "So, who's flying this crate?"

"I am," replied Landon.

"You are?!!" Roger exclaimed. "You didn't tell me that. I'm not going."

"Will you get your ass aboard?" Landon retorted.

"'Colonel Landon! I am here!" Milifi approached now, having made it after all.

"Excellent," remarked Landon. "Please, get aboard, Professor." Soon, they had departed the station and were on their way down to the planet. Routinely, the flight should take about twenty-five minutes.

About ten minutes after the shuttle departed, the orbital station lost communication with them. In ops, Major Ellsworth had Mr. Preston try to raise them again. "This is Orbital 129 to Shuttle 1, please respond, over."

No response. It was the fifth unsuccessful attempt. "Nothing, sir. There's just too much interference," said Preston.

"Major Ellsworth?" Lt. Miller from Long Range Optics had relocated to main ops so he could link his imaging instrumentation and telemetry directly to the command center. "You should see this, sir."

"Main view screen please, Lt. Miller," said Ellsworth.

A large screen mounted on the wall next to the commo alcove flashed to life. Miller punched up the rerouted L.R.O. images. The screen instantly displayed the distant, dark rift in space, still pulsing with shades of blue and violet. But something new appeared to be developing. Linear strings of deep twinkling red beads were appearing in the heart of the thing and washing outward.

Ellsworth suddenly had a realization. "Full magnification," he snapped. He had seen these images before. Where? The officer's academy? High School? He knew what this phenomenon was. It struggled to break through from his subconscious memory.

Miller punched up a more magnified view. The twinkling red beads separated now, single points of light resembling twirling red X's. Ellsworth's voice lost it's volume now, as he spoke in a near-whisper. "Oh, my God. The Celestial Event."

All eyes in ops turned to the screen. "You're right," agreed a female officer. Every high school kid learned about it in History Class. They'd all seen the video images.

Mr. Preston came out of his alcove. "I don't believe it." He stared in awe at the screen. "The 'Great Light Show of 2012.'"

Lots of kids had spent some time fascinated, some even obsessed, with this ever-unexplained incident. Will Preston had been one of those kids in high school, but hadn't given it much thought in years, until now, as it stared him in the face.

"I'll be damned," he said, unsure if he should be fascinated all over again, or scared to death.

"Sir," said Lt. Miller, "the incoming telemetry would seem to indicate that those red blips are…vessels."

Fascination did transform then, for everyone in ops, and everyone else on the station near a view port. "Vessels?" asked Ellsworth.

"Hundreds of thousands of them, sir," replied the stoic Miller.

"Can you lock down the range?" asked Ellsworth.

"Long range probes and relays…out of commission."

"Too much interference?"

"No, sir," said Miller, "I believe the entire battery has been destroyed. L.R.O. computer estimates range of unidentified vessels at .0049 light-years, which is 414.5988 *relative* A.U.'s." The estimation put the phenomenon and the glowing red vessels well outside the system, but still well before the comet reservoir, or local Oort cloud, defining the outer boundary of the NY-494 planetary system's gravitational influence. 'Just up the road a piece' in space terms.

"That's freaking close," said Ellsworth.

As they watched the L.R.O. screen, there was a series of stuttered jumps, and a small group of the twinkling red vessels leaped forward at them, spanning twice the distance of the system's heliopause in less than three seconds. Nine of the vessels now ringed the orbital station and three others peeled off and decelerated to streak towards the planet's surface.

One of the unknowns sat stationary directly in front of the operations center's massive view port, hanging less than a hundred meters from the station. The officers and techs present were eerily calm and quiet.

"Chief Kassab, status of shields?" asked Ellsworth, without turning away from the view port.

"Shields are at maximum strength, sir," an ops officer answered from a station behind him.

Ellsworth eyed the vessel that was nose-to-nose with the station, rubbing his chin. The intense red glow seemed to be some type of containment field, enveloping a ship within, but no details of the vessel inside were visible. The field itself radiated strangely, up close resembling fluid crystal.

Just then, a fanned out, laser-like beam shot out from the energy field, flickering on and off in a series of color shades. "Sir," said Chief Kassab, "I believe it is trying to find a wave-length to penetrate our shields."

Then, a sturdier flash seemed to lock on. The entire station interior was awash in the eerie red glow now, and a sound like shorting electrical wires reverberated through every deck. Then the beam abruptly switched off.

"What just happened?" asked Major Ellsworth.

"I believe we have just been scanned, sir," replied Kassab.

"Do we still have short-range sensors?"

"Affirmative, sir," replied the Chief.

"Well, then, Chief, scan them back," said Ellsworth.

Kassab activated the sensors, but could not penetrate the vessel's outer energy field. The pulsing red craft promptly fired another unknown type of beam at a point somewhere above the view port. There was a muffled rumble somewhere and the entire station trembled.

"Sir," said Kassab, "shield grids seventeen-bravo through seventeen-tango are down…standby…short-range sensor array has been destroyed."

"Damn," said the major. "Did you have time to get anything at all on them?"

"Only data on the containment field enveloping the vessel, sir," Kassab replied. "It appears to be…an anti-matter containment field."

"An anti-matter containment field around the entire vessel," Ellsworth echoed. "It doesn't make sense."

He was getting pissed. He walked over to stand beside the tactical systems officer. "Lt. Werner, activate defensive systems and standby on pulse guns."

The left side of the station's console lit up, and, just as quickly, the unknown fired another shot, promptly destroying the station's weapons arrays and taking out another section of the shield grid.

"Son-of-a-bitch," grumbled Ellsworth. "It would seem they have the advantage."

Now it was just a matter of waiting to see what happened next. And the U.S.S. King and the other ships of it's cruiser group were still about fourteen hours away.

The shuttle was through the planet's upper atmosphere, on it's way down. Warrant Officer Carter Willis tried communications again. "Shuttle 1 to Orbital 129, do you read me, over?" He waited, but there was no reply. "Nothing, sir," he said to Landon, next to him in the pilot's seat.

Suddenly, a glowing red object came alongside them, on the shuttle's port side, matching their speed. Everyone on board watched the pulsing light through the view ports.

Roger Hunt's eyes were wide and round as he watched the thing. "What the hell is that?"

"Oh, boy," said Landon. "This day just keeps getting weirder and weirder."

He banked the shuttle, attempting some obligatory evasive maneuvers. The unknown stayed with them. With a bright flash, a beam locked onto them, the eerie red plasma-like glow sweeping the interior of the shuttle as the alien vessel scanned them.

In an instant, the beam flicked off and the vessel fired on them, destroying the ship's defensive weapons and knocking out it's entire shield grid.. But the shuttle, less resilient than the station in orbit, was badly damaged in the exchange.

Sparks popped and spewed from a compartment towards the rear of the shuttle's interior. The controls stiffened in his hands and the ship became slow to respond to coaxing. What sounded like one of the field generators moaned and whined, threatening to overload or just shut down altogether, unable to decide which.

"Oh, man," said Landon, "we are in deep *doo-doo!*"

"That's one way of putting it," agreed Willis, trying to divert some power to where it was needed and still leave Landon enough to fly the ship. Still, the alien vessel stayed right with them.

"Nate, please tell me you can land this thing," said Roger Hunt.

Landon turned to Willis beside him and could only shrug. "No sweat, Roger, old buddy. I can get us down. We just won't be able to take off again."

Professor Milifi chimed in now, his voice pitched a little higher than usual. "I will be happy if we can be alive to deal with that problem later, 'Colonel. For now, I would like very much to be on the ground."

"I'm trying to get us there, Professor," said Landon, fighting the uncooperative controls. "As long as that thing doesn't blow us out of the sky, I think I can land safely."

Willis eyed him again, but Landon could only offer another shrug.

"Remind me to never fly with you again," said Roger.

"Funny," remarked Landon, "I don't remember twisting your arm."

Just then, the alien accelerated, streaking off toward the horizon. Breaking through the cloud ceiling, Landon had the science station in sight now. And a few kilometers beyond, the glowing red light had joined two others just like it, the three vessels now hovering on station above a wide, open plane in the distance.

Miles Merriweather and the other members of his site team stared dumbstruck at the three pulsing red orbs hovering in the sky above them. "Oh, my God," he murmured. "It's happening now. They're here."

The three vessels pulsed together uniformly, each swell of red glare like three slowly windmilling, twinkling X's in the sky. "Who's here?" asked a wary Charlie Pearson. "What are you on about, Miles?"

"Think, Charlie," said Merriweather. "Look at those lights. You know they're alien spacecraft. And look at the anomaly." He pointed at the growing rift, visible out in deep space, throbbing blue and violet. He turned to look at everyone present in turn. "We've all seen this before."

Not understanding what his young colleague was getting at, Pearson was prepared to argue that he was jumping to unfounded conclusions. But Dori Prideux stopped him. She at last understood what Merriweather had spent his life pursuing. "He's right, Charles. Those are alien ships. And we have all seen this before."

Thedo Vandenhoek now made the connection as well. The twinkling red X's, the distant, colorful rift in space. "The Celestial Event of 2012," he said.

Finally, Merriweather could see in Pearson's eyes that he, too, understood now. All of them did. But they didn't know whether they should congratulate Merriweather for being right, or run screaming for their lives.

Merriweather pointed out the glowing sphere in the sky which was the system's other planet, the big gas giant. "That's NY-494-Beta. In opposition alignment, just like Jupiter was on December 2nd, 2012." A million new possibilities flooded the young scientist's mind. "And if I'm right...oh, my god, we have to get out of here, right now."

He turned to Natalie Plant. "Natalie, start the bus! We have to go now!"

"Miles, dear boy, calm down," said Pearson. "Even if they are alien vessels, they don't appear to be hostile. They just seem to be observing us."

"It's not them I'm worried about," said Merriweather. "Don't you see, Charlie? These guys," he pointed at the glowing red orbs, "they're just scouts, an advance party."

"Advance party for what?" asked Carrie Blakely, a young brunette research assistant. She looked frightened.

"Listen," Merriweather tried to slow down so the others could catch up. "I never dreamed I'd actually see this happening. I just...noticed a lot of common factors about some sites that shouldn't be so coincidental, and some similarities in natural cycles, between our solar system and this one. But, I never dreamed it would happen in my lifetime. And if I'm right, in the middle of that rift is a...'phased' brown dwarf star."

He paused, waiting for Pearson to get his head around the idea. Merriweather had never related this aspect of his hypotheses to Pearson or anyone else.

"What is a brown dwarf, exactly?" asked the tech, Vandenhoek.

Carrie Blakely spoke up at this point. "A brown dwarf is a star that can't sustain nuclear fusion at it's core because it doesn't have sufficient mass. It's like an unlit star, so we can't see it." She, too, was quite intrigued now by Merriweather's ideas.

"A 'phased' brown dwarf star?" asked the incredulous Pearson. "What do you mean by 'phased?'"

"Like...there's an unstable wormhole that rotates around the galaxy in a regular cycle," Merriweather attempted to explain. "And it's dragging the brown dwarf around with it, each stop coinciding with several different cycles being aligned within a particular star's system. And I think the magnetic fields of massive gas giant planets play an important role in location and timing."

Dori began to understand, but still wasn't exactly sure what he meant. "But, why a brown dwarf?" she asked.

Then it hit Pearson, and he did understand where his young colleague was going. It was he who answered her question. "Because the gravitational effect of a nearby brown dwarf would explain certain things about our own solar system that we were never able to. The unexplained gravitational effect on the Oort cloud comets, and the orbit of Sedna. But after we traveled into space and found no brown dwarf, science abandoned the theory."

"But," interjected Blakely now, "for the brown dwarf to have a long-term effect on, say, Sedna, or comets, wouldn't it have to stay permanent, in a fixed orbit?"

"That's what you mean by 'phased,'" said Pearson now. "It's out of phase with our reality. No wonder we never found it. Quantum Field Physics," he explained, "particle exchange between two quantum fields."

"Or, in this case," Dori clarified, "between two dimensions."

"So who are they?" asked Natalie Plant, nodding at the hovering, twinkling red orbs.

Pearson eyed Merriweather now, the gears turning in his head. "Brown dwarfs have been discovered with planets orbiting them," he said.

"Well, like I said," responded Merriweather, "I think they're just scouts. There's something coming, something big. And I believe it will land...right here."

Pearson had the big picture now. "Natalie, perhaps you'd better start the bus." He turned to everyone else. "I agree with Miles. We should leave this place, at once."

"What about the rover?" asked Natalie.

"We'll have to leave it," said Pearson. "With the sonic emitters down it won't be safe traveling in an open vehicle."

"Give me three minutes," said Merriweather. "I have to get my notes."

Pearson didn't like it. "You can't possibly mean to go outside! It's not safe, Miles. Besides, those stampeding antelope-things have probably wrecked your lab."

"Three minutes," insisted Merriweather.

"I'll go with him," said Vanderhoek, loading a cartridge magazine into a high-powered rifle he had removed from a locker in back.

6.

Lt. Jones, Lopez, and Bailey had seen the glowing red orbs streak by, as if following the course of the road to a point beyond the jungle to hover, stationary. They were quickly joined by a third one.

"'Looks like they're directly above Merriweather's site," the Lieutenant said.

"Shit," said Lopez in disgust. "Are we sure we still want to go that way?"

"It's only about another kilometer," Jones said. "And in my book, that beats ten kilometers back through that jungle. Are you forgetting that thing that rolled us over and killed Norwood? There's a lot of other animals out here even more dangerous. And they won't stop just because you run into the…"

A tan blur erupted from the jungle and tackled Lopez, rolling with him in the dust, vicious snarls amid agonized screams. Watching in horror as the big cat mauled their friend, Jones and Bailey both raised their weapons but were afraid they'd hit Lopez.

"We have to get right up on it!" shouted Jones, moving forward now intending to jam the muzzle of his light machinegun into the creature's ribs and squeeze the trigger.

Before Bailey could move, he heard a rustle in the thick vegetation, caught a blur of movement. He whirled to his right and fired. The burst caught another of the animals at point blank range, killing it just as it was about to spring.

Another came out of the jungle after Jones, diverting his attention. He turned and fired. The animal dropped on the dusty road. When Jones turned again, the other big cat was loping away into the dense bush, dragging a very dead Lopez with it.

Bailey was shaking, visibly, as Jones turned to him. "We've got to get going, Bailey," said Jones, evenly. "Focus, soldier." He eyed the jungle on each side of the road. "There could be more of them right now, in there watching us."

Bailey's eyes now scanned the jungle, too. He set his jaw then, his trembling seeming to subside some. He glanced skyward again at the three winking red orbs hovering above their destination. It would be dark within a couple of hours. "Alright, L.T. Let's go."

Back at the science station, 'Colonel Landon had managed to land the stricken shuttle. Upon investigating the damage, his earlier assessment had proven very accurate. They wouldn't be taking off again. In fact, one of the station maintenance personnel had told him he was lucky to even have landed.

The camp around him seemed to be in a state of complete panic and chaos. The commo shack, which had also housed the pulsed signal generator and several scientific monitoring stations, was a twisted, smoldering wreck. Soldiers with fire hoses were attempting to put out the last of the flames. Mirc troops had set up a series of sandbag defensive emplacements, and were manning a loose perimeter about a hundred-fifty feet inside the fourteen-foot high chain link fence that ran around the compound.

The landing party had figured out the situation pretty quickly upon climbing out of the shuttle. The sonic emitters were down, and a horde of frenzied animals appeared to be assaulting the fence, as if fleeing something and believing they'd be safe inside the compound. Scores of small, panicked primates had already climbed over the fence and scurried in different directions, shrieking and adding to the havoc.

But the soldiers in the defensive positions ignored them for the most part. They had more dangerous problems to worry about. The big predatory cats with the odd manes had figured out that they could leap over the fence.

Five of them had already been shot dead when they came over, one making it as far as the cafeteria where it was able to maul a tech to death before it could be put down. Now every time one approached the fence it was warned back with a round of weapons-fire. But in the expanse of the cleared buffer zone outside the fence as many as twelve more still prowled warily around. Some took out their frustration on the hapless monkey and lemur-like creatures pouring out of the jungle. But still others clearly wanted in, pacing around just at the jungle's edge, eyeing the soldiers through the fence.

A Mircom Corporal approached the landing party now as they stood on the pad taking in the scene around them. He saluted Landon, who returned it. "'Colonel, I've been instructed to escort you to the Command Post." He turned to Captain Hernandez. "The Arms Room is there also, Ma'am, if you'd like to draw a sidearm."

As the group headed off following the Corporal away from the pad, Landon quickened his pace to come alongside him. "What the hell happened to the commo shack?"

The Corporal pointed to the glowing red lights, eleven kilometers distant. "When the first two unknowns came over, the pulsed signal generator was active, trying to get a signal out. One of them destroyed the shack."

"How many casualties?" Landon asked.

'We're not sure yet, sir," replied the Corporal.

"Is Lt. Jones at the Command Post?" he asked the young soldier.

"No, sir. Lt. Jones left this morning leading a team to make contact with Dr. Merriweather's party. We haven't had contact with either group since. Lt. Allen is in command of the C.P."

A loud, banging clamor from the direction of the main gate caught everyone's attention. When they turned to look, Roger Hunt and Professor Milifi both froze in their tracks, taking in a huge pachyderm of some sort, with a huge, flat, upper forehead which it was apparently not shy about lowering to use as a battering ram at a dead run, which is what the animal was doing now to the front gate. It hung nearly decimated, on mangled hinges. Once more and the beast would be in the compound, where it could and would most certainly bulldozer over anything or anyone that might be in it's path.

The soldiers accompanying the landing party were behind Milifi and Hunt now. "Sirs?" said one. "Could you keep moving please?"

Their feet began moving again, and they hurried to catch up to the others, but still watching in horror the scene unfolding at the gate. The troops who'd been manning the bunkers covering the gate were ordered to fall back, and were doing so with great enthusiasm.

The pachyderm juggernaut came snorting and bellowing through the gate behind them, trampling it beneath it's pile-driver feet. From a nearby sandbag emplacement a soldier fired a rocket-propelled grenade. The projectile sailed over the animal's back and exploded in the fence. The soldiers could be heard shouting and cursing on the perimeter.

They laid down a fierce volley of fire as the beast charged the defensive positions. They had reloaded the grenade launcher and another rocket streaked toward it's target, this time finding it's mark. The explosion finished the animal off.

As the landing party entered the Mircom Command Post, Second Lieutenant Nigel Allen was barking orders to the perimeter troops over his head-set. "I know the gate is down! Just make sure nothing else gets through it!"

"Lieutenant?" Landon called from behind him.

Allen whirled on him, rendering a quick salute when he realized who he was. "Lt. Nigel Allen, sir. I'm Lt. Jones's Executive Officer. Do you wish to take command of the C.P. at this time?"

"That won't be necessary, Lieutenant." Landon wondered quietly how the orbital station was faring.

A soldier came in from outside. "Lieutenant! You'd better come take a look at this, sir."

Nearly everyone crowded out of the Command Post to see for themselves this newest development. All eyes turned to the sky. A gigantic object was drifting slowly down from the sky, enshrouded in the same deep red glow that encased the winking orbs, but much more massive, and with an almost discernible outline within, like the spired pinnacles of a mountain-sized castle or citadel.

Dumbfounded, they watched the huge object descend. The chaos that had gripped the camp seemed suddenly to hush. The sporadic weapons-fire abruptly ceased, and even the frenzied animals quieted, flowing now in a wave around the outside of the fence, like a stream around a protruding stone. They had given up on getting in or through the outpost in the path of their flight. They just wanted to be far away from the gigantic thing landing in the distance.

7.

Lt. Jones and Spec. 4 Bailey made their way up the middle of the road with winged feet, each warily watching the jungle on their side, weapon at the ready. And every few hurried steps one or the other would turn to check behind them. Though they had seen no more animals since they'd been ambushed by the big panthers and Lopez was dragged into the jungle, they felt as if something had been stealing along with them just out of sight, stalking them, waiting for it's moment. They were certain something was watching them.

Then they noticed that the twinkling red orbs overhead slowly began moving. For quite a while they had hovered above in a straight line, pulsing in perfect unison. But now they slowly began spreading their formation in three different directions, one coming right up the road toward them.

And then they saw it over the tops of the jungle trees. Like a colossal, floating palace, encased in fluid crystal that glowed deep red, like pure light. "What the fuck?" Bailey could barely mouth the words. They stopped in their tracks. That gravity-defying mountain was going to land directly on Merriweather's site.

Then they heard something approaching from ahead of them. The sound was faint at first, indiscernible. It could have been the up and down braying of another of this planet's crazy animals, they couldn't be sure. But it was definitely getting louder. Then, on the road ahead it burst around a bend.

It was the big bus the scientists used to stay out at the site, barreling straight at them. Never so happy to see anything in their lives, they began waving their arms in the air. That big, glorious bus! They'd be safe on the bus.

The woman in the driver's seat stood on the brakes, bringing the big vehicle to a sliding stop in front of them. She motioned frantically through the big windshield for them to hurry on board. As they dashed for the safety of the bus, they could see the handful of passengers on board peering out at them.

Lt. Jones flung the door open and they clambered hurriedly up the steps. Bailey wasted no time securing the door behind him. "Man, are we glad to see you guys!" he said.

But the words were lost in the explosive sound of the imploding windshield. A massive creature was reared in front of the bus, like a giant land eel, but with lizard-like legs spaced along it's sinews like a centipede. It's head looked like a giant snake with a large hooked beak, which it had slammed against the windshield, causing it to fall inward, pinning the driver in her seat.

The creature pulled it's skittering coils into the road now, looking to be at least forty feet long. The lizard's claws it now used to extract the ruined, flopping windshield panel, which it cast aside.

"NATALIE!" shrieked Carrie Blakely.

The windshield out of the way now, the big beak snaked in through the opening and snatched Natalie Plant out of the driver's seat with a crunch. Blood splashed everywhere.

Carrie Blakely was still screaming. Lt. Jones bellowed with nonsensical rage, producing two fragmentation grenades, pulling the pins and hurling them at the creature through the opening. "Get down," he shouted.

As everyone tried to duck, the grenades exploded. But the creature had coiled away, rearing back a great distance after snatching Natalie. It took a great deal of shrapnel, but it wasn't dead. Hissing loudly, the wounded eel-thing coiled tightly in on itself, then unwound sliding back into the jungle.

The road clear once more, no one objected when Lt. Jones, covered in Natalie Plant's blood, hopped in the driver's seat and got the bus moving again. And he wasn't stopping for anything.

At the science station, they had managed to get an accountability of personnel. The only person who had been present in the commo shack when the aliens destroyed it was Sgt. Hackett. He had been operating the pulsed signal generator, trying to get a message to the orbital station.

Scotty Price sat on a bench in the cafeteria, his friends, Julie Burlington and Bong-hwa Shim, sitting closely on either side of him. "That Sergeant died because of me," he said. He was numbed with guilt. "Because my Morse Code was rusty. For no reason at all. It should have been me."

"Scotty, you can't think like that, bro'," said Shim.

"The aliens destroyed the commo shack," Burlington added, trying to calm him, "not you."

Others around him who knew what he was going through tried to console him. Scotty was well-liked by everyone. Even some of the Mircom personnel came by and put a hand on his shoulder.

After the gigantic craft had landed out on the plane, one of the pulsing red orbs had shown up and parked itself in the sky directly above the station. No one dared guess what might happen next. It was nearly dark now, the sun barely visible hanging below the horizon. It appeared to be a waiting game.

Landon and the rest of his party, along with Lt. Allen and a couple other officers from the C.P. had all relocated to the open air observation tower. From there they had a pretty good vantage point of the huge ship with a telescope. But nothing had happened since it landed. It just sat out there, the red pulsing glow strobing in perfect unison not only with the smaller orbs hovering above the surface, but with all the red twinkling lights on the fringe of the distant rift in space.

"Wait, I think I see something," said a lieutenant holding a pair of binoculars. "It's the science bus."

The big bus came rocketing up the road leaving a plume of dust lingering in it's wake. Very quickly, it entered the compound, bouncing recklessly over the trampled gate. It finally slid to a halt in front of the cafeteria.

The personnel congregated inside the building began spilling out, eager to see what was happening. The bus passengers piled hurriedly out of the vehicle. They looked like they'd been through hell, a couple of them covered in blood. The front of the bus was scorched as though something had exploded directly in front of it, it's windshield missing.

Leaving a couple of observers posted in the tower, 'Colonel Landon and the others hurried to the ground to talk with them. As Landon made his way towards the parked bus he suddenly had an odd realization that the lovely Captain Martina Hernandez was at his side, and that they had been nearly attached at the hip since he'd managed to land the damaged shuttle. It seemed as if the intensity of this whole experience had finally created an accessible opportunity that perhaps both of them had desperately yearned for, an opportunity for them to finally form a bond.

He glanced into her eyes then, as she walked beside him. And the warmth he saw there assured him that, as horrible as this mess was, it had been just what they'd needed to throw them together. No matter what else happened, one good thing would survive this nightmare.

Landon heard Roger Hunt on the other side of him now. "Good lord, look at them."

Like Roger, Landon shuddered to think what they'd all been through. The two groups converged. There was going to be a lot of conferring and debriefing to do, an essential exchange of ideas and information.

Carrie Blakely was severely traumatized. She and Natalie Plant had been best friends. Julie Burlington stepped forward from the cafeteria on-lookers and led her to the infirmary to be examined. After assuring no one else needed medical attention, Landon suggested they all move into the cafeteria.

Once inside, the meeting of minds quickly got underway. Landon and the other officers listened intently as, under a barrage of questions from Professor Milifi, Merriweather attempted to relate his theories in their simplest form, easy-to-grasp and to the point. Now and then, Charlie Pearson thought of simpler terms and helped him out where he could.

Landon thought he had the gist of it, but the question then remained, "How do we get the priority systems back on line? The sonic emitters? Communications?" he asked Merriweather.

The young scientist pondered the point blank question for a moment, then shook his head. "We don't," he finally responded. "We're not getting through the interference. The red glow around these objects is anti-matter containment. You see, the data that translated as an increase in background radiation was both right and wrong. The background radiation of our universe is constant. It's the signature of the Big Bang. It can neither increase nor decrease. The disturbance itself is an exchange of particles at a micro-wave level. The particles from their universe are anti-matter. Only an undetectable phase barrier is preventing the 'annihilation' of particles from our universe meeting the anti-particles from their universe."

"'Annihilation?'" asked Roger Hunt. He didn't like the sound of that.

"A very…'big bang,'" clarified Pearson, coining a phrase.

Merriweather continued. "Behind this phase barrier, in the rift, there must be, like, a buffer zone, where some particles actually do meet, like a giant anti-matter reactor, and the energy created in the reaction manifests as photons, gamma rays. That's where the visual effect comes from. The 'light show' within the rift. Your sensors penetrated this phase barrier and read the increased energy as background radiation."

Landon turned to Captain Hernandez, who nodded her agreement. "That's what I was trying to tell you this morning," she said.

He glanced at Professor Milifi. "And you as well, I believe, Professor."

Milifi smiled and nodded.

"But," Merriweather seemed to be concentrating on something that puzzled him, "obviously these aliens are able to manipulate matter and anti-matter at will," he paused waiting for his brain to answer a question for him. Then it hit him. "That's it! It really is…a 'light show.' It's all for aesthetics."

Then, an idea occurred to Dori Prideux. "It almost seems as though this is all some type of ritual ceremony for these beings, or perhaps a festival."

"Okay," said Lt. Jones, who had cleaned up and changed coveralls. "So, if these aliens have visited us before, right in our own backyard, as you say, during the Celestial Event back in 2012, why are they so hostile now? Why didn't they attack us way back then? Where we lived?"

"Maybe because they didn't consider us a threat then," said Merriweather.

"And because," interjected Dori, "they did not land on Earth in 2012, did they, Miles?"

"No," he replied. "They landed on Mars, instead, probably to avoid contact with us. In 2012, there was no one on Mars."

"No offense, Dr. Merriweather," said Lt. Jones, "but how does any of this help our situation?"

Merriweather looked confused. He thought they all understood. "Don't you see? In 2012, this...visitation lasted exactly twenty-four hours and thirty-seven minutes, the exact length of a Martian day."

Landon was beginning to understand what he was getting at. "So, you're saying..."

" If I'm right," confirmed Merriweather, "this should all be over soon. They'll probably just leave."

Landon glanced at Pearson and Milifi. "He's been right so far," Pearson offered.

There was a commotion of raised voices outside. Everyone headed for a window or door to look out. Landon and several others stepped outside. But what greeted them was an entirely new development.

A brilliant red beam shot from the massive vessel that had landed eleven kilometers away to the pulsing red orb directly above the station. Something big was happening.

Landon turned to Merriweather, standing beside him. "And where, Doctor, in your grand scheme of things, does this fit in?"

Merriweather hesitated. "Uh, it doesn't."

The molten red beam from the big ship in the distance remained in place, connected to the smaller vessel above the science station, but seemed suddenly to stabilize, or lock. That background sizzling, high voltage electrical sound that had accompanied it's appearance dissipated, the irregular flickering of an anti-matter containment field trying to establish itself straightening rigidly and aligning only with the pulsing of every red-cloaked object in view.

"What's going on?" Landon murmured to Merriweather.

"Oh, man, I hope I'm wrong," the young scientist murmured.

Roger Hunt eyed him. "*Now* you hope you're wrong?"

"Something may be teleporting from there to here," said Merriwether.

"Lovely," said Landon.

Suddenly, a series of deep red beams fanned down from a point in the twinkling orb above, forming what could have been somehow liquefied or molten crystal, defining into a broad pyramid shape. It was another containment field. And something big, dark, and ugly seemed to be materializing within it.

Landon realized again that Martina was still at his side, and Merriweather was right. Something was paying them a visit. He turned to her, hurriedly, trying to shoo her away with gentle shoves. "Go," he said, "get the hell out of here!"

"Nope," she responded flatly. She wasn't budging.

Something began to take a loose shape within the containment field, and a sound like the distorted, time-tortured voices of the damned filled the air. Landon turned back to the apparition before them. Something black and billowing boiled inside the pyramid-shaped field, almost like thick smoke, but having mass, density, tar-like. The eerie caterwauling cacophony of voices rose, swelled, threatened to blow their eardrums out, then settled on a voice and a language.

In a rumbling, guttural bass tone, the voices unified into one. "Who speaks for you?" The very ground beneath their feet and air about them seemed to tremble in fear.

Landon gulped, whispering to Hernandez to get behind him. He stepped forward. "I guess that'd be me," he said aloud.

Faster than any of them could blink, a section of the glowing, pulsing red field shot forward, protruding to envelope him without actually touching him. Then it retracted back into place just as quickly.

"I know you," thundered the voice. "In long ages past, I knew your race."

"Sorry," offered Landon, "I guess I wasn't around then. What are you?"

The voice grew louder, more thunderous, as if offended now, slighted in some way. "I am of God!"

"Really?" remarked Landon. "That's quite a claim."

Professor Milifi stepped forward now to confront the alien. He seemed indignant, angry. Now it was he who had been offended. "No!" he proclaimed, pointing a finger at the thing defiantly. "You are a murderer! You are not of *my* God!"

"Then I am of your death!" thundered the voice.

A protrusion of the field shot forward to envelope Milifi, but this time it did not leave him untouched. Within the red glowing molten crystal, Milifi screamed and squirmed, the liquefied version of him dropping to it's knees, then dissolving into pure light and ultimately winking out. So that was annihilation.

In shock, Roger Hunt raised his shotgun as every Mirc soldier present raised their own weapons. Merriweather shouted, raising his hands before them.

"No!" he was pleading with them. "Don't fire! Do nothing to provoke it! Even if we could, we don't dare damage the containment field!"

"Who are you?" the voice snarled. It was angry now.

The young scientist raised his open hands, the only peaceful gesture he could think of. "I am Merriweather. I just study science. Who are you?"

The voice swelled to cyclone pitch. "I am Nibiru!"

And now, Merriweather, and perhaps Pearson, or Dori Prideux, understood. This was a word Merriweather knew from his research. It was ancient Sumerian.

The bellowing voice continued. "I am your Alpha and Omega! All must worship me!" The thing thundered a final reverberating proclamation, "I AM NIBIRU!"

The beams and containment field from overhead blinked out. The red beam connected to the distant colossal shape on the plane switched off. In awe, the on-lookers at the science station watched in silence as the massive vessel lifted off, eleven kilometers away. It accelerated quickly and shot away in the direction of the rift. No sooner had it vanished from view than several twinkling red orbs, including the one overhead, joined it, disappearing quickly in the depths of space. And when they had gone, the light show and the rift winked out.

Miles Merriweather earned an endless procession of accolades and awards in the many years life would grant him after this incident. His work in Physics was renowned ever after.

Charlie Pearson went on to publish ground-breaking theories in quantum field physics, but for the rest of his life, accredited Miles Merriweather for pointing out new possibilities and ideas to him.

Roger Hunt retired immediately following the incident, returning home to Earth, never to leave the planet again. He bought a big boat and opened a charter fishing service in Florida.

Six months after the incident at NY-494-Alpha, Nathan Landon and Martina Hernandez were married. They often traveled to Earth to charter Roger's boat. But, Roger of course never allowed them to pay.

At the science station, the day after the aliens had gone, Julie Burlington had cornered Scotty Price outside the Cafeteria. "'Still know where to get your hands on that bottle of tequila?"

"You know it, sweetie," he had of course responded.

"Be at my door in fifteen minutes," she instructed him.

"Well," he smiled his trademark smile. "This *is* a *Celestial Event.*"